BAD BLIND DATE

BILLIONAIRE'S CLUB BOOK 8

ELISE FABER

Elise Faber
SNARKY BOOKS FOR SNARKY MINDS

BAD BLIND DATE
BY ELISE FABER
Newsletter sign-up

This is a work of fiction. Names, places, characters, and events are fictitious in every regard. Any similarities to actual events and persons, living or dead, are purely coincidental. Any trademarks, service marks, product names, or named features are assumed to be the property of their respective owners, and are used only for reference. There is no implied endorsement if any of these terms are used. Except for review purposes, the reproduction of this book in whole or part, electronically or mechanically, constitutes a copyright violation.

BILLIONAIRE'S CLUB

Bad Night Stand

Bad Breakup

Bad Husband

Bad Hookup

Bad Divorce

Bad Fiancé

Bad Boyfriend

Bad Blind Date

Bad Wedding

Bad Engagement

ONE

Trix

SHE WATCHED HER FRIEND, Tanner, kiss his fiancée again then checked her watch, wondering two things.

First, why she'd come back to California in the first place.

And second, what the hell kind of drugs she'd been on when agreeing to this date in the first place.

The only good thing about it was that she had buffers: Tanner and his fiancée, Kelsey. Heather, her half-sister and the only decent member of her family, along with Heather's husband, Clay, who was pretty to look at and not *too* annoying.

For a man.

Probably not the best attitude to have going into a blind date, but she'd shown up, hadn't she?

Anyway, the dinner had also meant she'd been able to see Tanner. She'd met the photographer in sub-Saharan Africa almost five years before while she'd been working and he'd been documenting the health crisis for the Red Cross. They'd kept in touch, and he'd invited her to his wedding. It had been a surprise to both of them that they each knew Heather.

But that was the way the O'Keiths worked.

Infiltrating their way into everyone's lives.

Even if they didn't want it.

Regardless, she was back in California for the time being, ready to begin a new chapter in her life.

Apparently, that meant starting by dating.

At least, that was Heather's logic.

Or maybe Trix's own brand of stupid.

Still, whatever it was that had convinced her to come, she was there now and was going to make the best of it.

Or at least that *had been* her thought until she recognized who was approaching the table.

Him.

Trix slammed her eyes closed and counted to five.

It could *not* be him.

Could not—

She opened her eyes.

Clay was on his feet, shaking the man's hand, shaking *Jet's* hand, and making introductions all around. Heather looked thrilled, probably because Jet was gorgeous and funny and smart—

"And this is Heather's sister, Trix. She's a nurse."

Jet knew that.

Because he knew her. *Intimately.*

The doctor and the nurse. So cliché. So stupid on her part to think that things in her life might have turned out differently.

He'd been smiling as he turned to meet her, and it was almost comical to see his expression darken to fury. Or it *would* have, if that fury hadn't been directed at her. By then his hand was already in hers, mid-shake and *fuck* if his touch didn't still make sparks shoot down her arm.

She went to pull back, but he held fast then jerked her forward, as though he were giving her a hug in greeting.

No one at the table could see that he was hissing in her ear.

"What the fuck are you playing at, Trixie?"

She did some hissing of your own. "*Nothing*. I had no idea this date was you otherwise I sure as hell wouldn't have come," she snapped, ignoring the way his scent coiled her stomach, sending little tendrils of heat down between her thighs. "You're the last person I'd want to see at this table. And that includes my parents or maybe even Hitler, you freaking asshole."

"Trixie," he began.

"Fuck off, Jet," she said, then pulled back and plunked into her chair, not about to ruin everyone's night just because she couldn't stand the man she'd been set up with.

She'd endure.

It was what she did.

Jet sat down next to her, and she tried to force herself *not* to look.

She didn't succeed.

And what she saw on his face wasn't fury, not any longer. It was weariness.

Good. After what he'd done to her, she deserved a man treading around her with a bit of hesitation. She'd been hurt before—heartsick and sad, a few times even devastated—when her relationships had ended.

But Jet had broken her.

He was the *one* man she'd let in, with whom she'd shared her past and hopes, her pain and desires. So maybe he wouldn't understand how important what she'd shared was because she'd spent so long being closed down with everyone around her. Maybe he couldn't have realized how hard it had been for her to give what she'd given. But part of her felt like . . . he *should* have known. Especially since he'd shown about as much care with her exposed and vulnerable heart as a physician tossing a soiled bandage onto the floor.

For a nurse to pick up.

Because that was all she'd ever been to him.

A convenient place to stash his dick before he'd tossed her aside, dirty and used, and she had to cobble herself together enough to throw away those pathetic hopes she'd been hanging on to.

"Trixie," he murmured.

She smiled brightly and picked up the menu. "I've heard the prickly pear margaritas are delicious," she announced to the table at large.

As she knew it would, that turned the conversation to Kelsey, who had proclaimed her love of the cocktail far and wide as they'd all chatted a few minutes before. This jump-started the bantering with the table at large, and pretty soon, the waiter came over to take their orders.

All through dinner, she managed to keep the conversation light, to keep her physical and verbal distance from Jet while still pretending to get to know him enough to satisfy the others at the table.

Her fatal flaw began when she slipped away to use the bathroom.

Because when she came out, Jet was standing in the hall.

Sniffing, she started to move past him.

His hand on her arm stilled her.

"What, Jet?" she snapped. "What could you possibly have to say to me?"

A growl. "Nothing."

"Good."

"*Everything.*"

He kissed her, and the world went topsy-turvy.

TWO

Jet

IN FAIRNESS, the *smack* of Trixie's palm across his cheek was probably warranted.

They hadn't seen each other in nearly three years, not since he'd packed up and moved on to another assignment.

And part of the reason he'd packed up was because he'd known he'd never get what he needed from Trix.

Selfish? Yes.

The truth? Also, yes.

Cutting ties before he got even more connected, before it got even harder to leave? Painful, but necessary.

Trixie was beautiful. She was fun to be with, hilarious, and the most low-maintenance person he'd ever met. She didn't need anyone's help. She got her shit done and did it well.

Which had been part of the problem.

He hadn't felt needed, hadn't felt loved. He'd had scraps tossed his way or held back in reserve, and he *knew* he couldn't live with that.

He needed *more*.

And circling back to selfish. But look, he knew himself, knew how much he enjoyed being with Trix, but he also knew he couldn't have a future with a woman he felt shut out from, one who preferred to exist in two side-by-side lives rather than two intertwined ones. After his childhood, after spending so much time being shut out and trying—and failing—to earn his parents' love, Jet knew he couldn't go through that again.

It wasn't sustainable, and so he'd torn off the Band-Aid.

Quick and painless.

Of course, it had definitely been the first, just not the second.

But, back to the well-deserved smack. Trix shoved his chest hard, tearing her mouth from his, and skittering several steps away. "What the fuck is your problem?" she snapped, wiping the back of her hand across her lips. "I-I can't believe that you would think you had any right to touch me."

She was absolutely right. Not that he was going to tell her as much. "I just had to check on something."

Her teeth came together with a sharp *click*. "You're fucking unbelievable."

But he wasn't lying.

The rest of the table had cleared out while Trix had been using the restroom, ostensibly because they had work and life commitments, but Jet knew they'd been trying to give him and Trix some time alone, based on the knowing look that Clay had given him before his friend and Heather had taken off. Tanner was a cool guy, and his girl, Kelsey, had been a hoot. They'd both preceded Heather and Clay, Kelsey's cheeks flushed from the sheer volume of prickly pear margaritas she'd consumed over the course of the meal.

Based on the hot glances she'd been shooting Tanner as they'd prepared to leave, the other man was going to have a good night.

Unlike him.

"I was checking on you," he said. "Not whether we still had enough heat between us to spontaneously combust. Though"—he leaned back against the wall, crossing his ankles and arms—"in case you were wondering. We do."

Trix rolled her pretty gray eyes. "As I mentioned previously, you're fucking unbelievable."

Jet grinned. "Thanks."

"Not a compliment, fuck twit," she muttered, brushing by him and heading back to the table, not knowing the rest of the group had already left.

He trailed her, and because he was a total asshole already, he figured he might as well enjoy the view. And it was a *view*. Tight black dress, pointy heels she could stab him with, full sleeve of tattoos down both arms visible.

Jet had spent many an hour holding Trix close and studying those swirling colorful pictures, tracing them with his fingers.

Now she stopped, those arms falling to her sides as she took in the empty table.

Slowly, she turned, angry eyes coming up to meet his.

He held out her purse.

Two steps and she came close. Fire in her gaze, fury in her stride. One part of him thought she was going to smack him again, another thought she might kiss him when those gray eyes caught on his mouth before drifting up to meet his eyes.

The air in his lungs caught.

Fuck, yes. He'd had a taste and now he wanted more—that brief touch had been enough for him to crave her lips on his for a hell of a lot longer than a few seconds.

She leaned close . . . and snatched the purse from his hands.

Then spun around and high-tailed it for the front doors.

And he was again in the not-so-unfortunate position of having to follow her out.

Trix could *move* in those heels, *click-clacking* across the floor, pushing out the doors, ass bouncing as she strode to her car. Conveniently, the small gray hybrid was parked right next to his sedan.

She beeped the locks, yanked at the handle, and tossed her purse inside.

A sheet of dark brown hair flew over her shoulder as she spun to face him again. "Why the fuck are you following me?" she snapped then threw her arms wide. Jet noticed there was a new addition to the inside of her left arm—a curved line that was shaded with blue and purple. But before he could look closer, she let her hands fall to her sides. "This is your chance to go. So take it. We both know you're excellent at it."

He'd been amused up until that point.

But her words struck home, and as such, his temper spiked.

He crowded her against the car, close enough that he could smell the slightly tropical scent of her shampoo. Even in the middle of the jungle, with humidity making all the rest of them smell like ass, she'd still been all coconut and vanilla and pineapple.

Like a fucking piña colada and he'd been thirsty.

"I didn't *want* to leave," he growled, leaning in and inhaling that tropical scent into his lungs.

"More. Fucking. Lies."

"I *had* to go."

"Great." She shoved at his chest. "Sure. So, if you *had* to go, then why were you so pissed off to see me at the table?"

She had him there.

But he'd been pissed because he'd been blindsided at seeing her. He'd left three years before and then spent the entire time trying to pretend she hadn't existed at all, and now he was finally moving on with his life and had agreed to go on a fucking date after a long ass hiatus, *and* then of course, it had been Trix sitting at that table waiting for him.

Beautiful, fun, smart Trixie had been there.

Reminding him of everything he'd walked away from.

He ignored the fact that he'd initially felt a blip of pleasure at her presence then narrowed his eyes and focused on the knee-jerk pain of knowing that no matter what he did, what he gave, she wouldn't ever be able to meet him in the middle . . . and so he said something unforgivable, "I was pissed that you were flaunting your tits to the world in that dress."

Her cheeks flared pink. "How *dare* you," she gritted, shoving him back enough to sink down into the driver's seat. "How *fucking* dare you. As if you think you have some sort of say in my body, in my clothes."

She wasn't wrong.

He was just trying to be an asshole. To push her away like she'd pushed him, to keep her at a distance and remind himself of all the reasons she was wrong for him.

So he wouldn't forget all the bad and remember the good.

Trix in his bed, smiling up at him.

Trixie working alongside him, unfazed at whatever crisis thrown their way and always finding a way to get through it without losing her smile.

Trix who'd seen so much, and who'd always had his back.

Who'd never judged.

So, yes, insinuating that about her clothes, about her as a woman, was a low fucking blow.

But it was easier to despise Trix for that initial pulse of joy upon seeing her, easier to blame the fact that their relationship had been doomed from the start on her because she was so closed off and unavailable and—

"Oof."

Strong.

Caught in the past, he wasn't prepared for her shove. He stumbled back enough for her to slam the driver's door shut. He heard the locks click, the engine start up, then had to jump another pace back when she hit the gas and screeched out of the spot.

The glare she shot him as she pulled out made him glad he hadn't jumped in front of the car to stop her.

Because she wouldn't have stopped.

And he couldn't help but think that maybe he deserved it.

In many ways.

THREE

Trixie

SHE WAS RUNNING on about two hours of sleep and a half-cup of coffee because she'd gone on a fucking blind date the evening before instead of grocery shopping . . . and still needed to show up on time for her shift.

But that was nothing new.

She'd spent a decade working abroad, moving from country to country in under-supplied and sometimes dangerous conditions, often with a limited amount of caffeine.

Definitely not the way she preferred to work.

But she could push through.

She *always* pushed through.

Sighing, she tugged her scrub top over the long-sleeved shirt she'd slipped on, then pulled on and zipped up her hospital-branded fleece. Feet into sneakers, hair into a ponytail, home-made lunch in her purple insulated case, and she was ready to go.

Before she'd moved to San Francisco three months before, or rather before she'd moved to a town *south* of San Francisco—

because working for a nonprofit didn't exactly make a girl rich—she hadn't worked at an actual hospital for years. Now, she'd adjusted to her job. For the most part.

She still missed the kids.

The innocent smiles and the excitement when they came to help.

The ones here weren't terrible, but most of them also didn't know how good they had it.

She knew how good she had it.

Money hadn't been flush when she'd been a kid, even as an O'Keith—or well, she'd technically been a Donovan since her mom hadn't taken the O'Keith name. Regardless, her father might be a billionaire and the owner of a Fortune 500 company, and her sister, Heather, might be the newest named female billionaire in the world, but Trix wasn't in that circle. She had been part of his second family, part of *her mother's taint* (and thanks dear old Dad for those kind words when she'd gone to ask him for help paying for medical school).

Look, she got it. Her mom was a disaster. Flighty, burned through money faster than water flowing through fingers. She was selfish and . . . frankly, she could be mean.

So, Trix hadn't exactly won the parent lottery.

The dream of medical school had disappeared, and she'd worked her way through nursing school instead.

Pivoting, adapting, *that* she could do.

And it wasn't like everyone could have everything, could they?

"Nope," she muttered, agreeing with her inner monologue while grabbing her backpack and heading for the door. "They can't have everything."

But at the very least, she could do something to make the world a little better for someone else.

Her shift had been relatively uneventful.

Or, at least, uneventful for the ED—emergency department —because there weren't any gunshot wounds or people threatening to stab her. There weren't any potentially scary cases that might be ebola or another highly communicable disease.

A broken arm, a heart attack, and one stab wound.

Not exciting.

Okay, so maybe she had a high tolerance for excitement, but they had thirteen beds and a full staff of nurses and doctors twiddling their thumbs.

It was making her crazy.

At least in the field she'd always had something to do, something to occupy her time with.

There weren't empty hours to think.

About a certain unnamed doctor.

Okay, fine.

About Jet and how good he'd been in bed—

No. That wasn't fair, either, because, yes, they'd been great in bed together, their bodies seeming like they were made for one another, but the entirety of their friendship, even before the brief interlude when they'd transitioned into lovers . . . *that* had been good.

She'd been in love and Jet . . .

She hadn't been enough.

Not surprising.

Trixie didn't have a self-worth issue. She knew she had value. She was smart and capable and good at her job. But she also wasn't soft or emotive or the type of woman that would clasp her hands and flutter her eyelashes and let her man know he was her hero.

She didn't need a hero.

She *needed* a partner.

She'd thought Jet had understood that, had thought he wanted the same in return. *Sigh*. She'd thought *a lot* of things, but her being what Jet wanted as a future had been perhaps the most grievous of her errors.

Well, obviously Trix had been wrong, and now it was time to move on. No time to cry over spilled milk or keep up all her teenage girl level sighing. Stifling another of the said exhalations, she headed to the break room. So what, Jet was around. Her life was busy and full. It wasn't like she was going to open herself to him again.

Been there. Done that. Got the souvenir balloon, and it had popped.

Lucky her.

Trix opened the lock on her locker and pulled on her backpack then straightened the arms on her fleece before grabbing her lunchbox.

Time to wade through some traffic, order takeout, and get caught up on about ten years of quality—and she had to be honest, some *not* quality—television. She was going to forget all about Jet and their past, forget how good it had felt when he'd touched and kissed and held her, forget about—

The man walked into the break room.

Dressed in a lab coat, stethoscope draped around his neck, he was talking to the chief trauma specialist, Tricia Heldway, and didn't notice her.

Thank God for small miracles.

She whipped around, facing her locker, and doing her best impression of a sidle as they spoke. Neither stopped their conversation as she approached the door, and she started to slip out, only to be halted when something caught her backpack.

When a *hand* caught her backpack.

Jet's chocolate eyes met hers. "Hey, Trix."

Tricia's head tilted to the side. "Oh, do you know, Trix, Jet? She's one of our best nurses."

Trixie tried to tug herself out of Jet's grip, but he didn't release her. In fact, he exerted inexorable pressure on her backpack that she ended up very near his side. Close enough that she could smell the spice of him, close enough to sense the coiled strength of power, close enough that she had to smother a shiver when she remembered how well he'd used that power.

The humid heat on their skin that had made their bodies stick together, the way he'd held her tight, his fingers almost bruising, the thin cushion of the mattress as he'd pounded into her.

The sounds of the jungle, the smell of smoke and ash from campfires.

Feeling so incredibly exhausted and yet exhilarated because they'd made a difference, trailed by the moments of feeling so damned low when they hadn't.

Such an intense time in her life, both with her career and with her heart.

And now she had come full circle.

Back trying to find her own path to making a difference . . . right alongside Jet.

Who replied to Tricia's question with a, "Yup, I know her."

Ringing endorsement, that.

But Tricia smiled anyway. "Well, I'll let you two catch up. I'm going to wrap up my charting and get out of here." She waved and left.

Trix tried to follow her. "I should—"

The grip on her backpack stayed firm. "You're working here."

She sighed, chin dropping to her chest as she debated whether to push it. "Yup," she eventually said, echoing his earlier reply. "For a couple months now."

He dropped his arm. "Cool."

Slowly, she inched away. "Cool." Another step. "'Kay, bye."

One half of that mouth curved up. "Okay, bye."

Trixie escaped into the hall, narrowly missing being mowed over by a gurney. She sent an apologetic wave and chagrined look toward the patient and her coworker's way. "Sorry," she muttered, plastering herself against the wall as they moved by. Once they were gone and she started moving again, she half-expected Jet's hand to snag her backpack and tug her to a stop a second time. It didn't.

She wasn't disappointed. Nope. She wasn't.

Definitely not.

And yet the sound of her internal derisive snort still rang in her ears as she hurried to her car.

Fucking Jet Hansen.

FOUR

Jet

HE RESISTED the urge to chase after Trix.

On one hand, she wasn't in her car, so the threat of him being run over was minimal. On the other, there were no shortage of sharps—syringes and scalpels came to mind—within reach, and she was well-versed in using them.

But that wasn't why he stayed in the break room, why he walked over to the water dispenser and downed a paper cup full instead of following her, why he stowed his valuables in a locker then his lunch in the fridge.

Because he couldn't risk getting attached again.

It was bad enough that she was in the same state, in the same hospital.

But he'd been burned by the flame that was Trix Donovan once, and that was enough.

Sighing, he stretched his neck, wondering how in all of the hospitals in the world, how after his stretch of doctoring all around the globe he'd ended up here. With Trix.

Some might say fate or kismet.

Others might say hell.

If the way his cock had twitched just watching Trix, he was definitely going with hell.

And with that fateful thought, Jet straightened his shoulders, pushed his dick and its twitching in the vicinity of the gorgeous brunette down, and focused on the work. Just like he'd done for the last three years.

Just like he was going to continue to do.

SEVEN IN THE morning came slower than he expected. Then again, the department hadn't been particularly busy, and he wasn't used to working nights.

Or working in a hospital setting rather than in the field.

One of his other physicians on shift that night had assured him the calm wouldn't last, that there would be a full moon, or it would rain and then people would be flocking to the ED, that in the meantime, he should enjoy the peace.

Jet wished he could.

But the itch under his skin wouldn't abate.

It wasn't like he'd been constantly busy while in Lebanon, Haiti, or Syria, though there had been days on end where he hadn't taken a break, where he'd worked until he could barely see straight . . . and still, the itch had been there.

Missing something.

Missing some*one*.

"Fuck," he muttered, knowing that he needed to adjust back to civilian life, to being back in this setting. He'd burned out, needed to live some place with running water and electricity and a good mattress.

Maybe he'd go back.

Maybe he'd serve for shorter-term deployments or in more domestic emergencies.

But for now, the idea of just being home was paramount.

Perhaps then he'd be able to move on with his life. He wasn't a perennial bachelor by choice. He wanted to be settled, to have a family, with kids and maybe a dog and cat.

Not a picket fence.

But he'd take a wrought iron one.

Grinning at his idiotic and sleep-addled mind, Jet made his way to his car. He'd put an obscene deposit down for a condo near the hospital, one that would have been impossible to make without the money his parents left him.

Money he'd promised himself he'd never use.

Money he'd used anyway.

But then again, a lot of his principles had changed over the last six years. He'd been young, only a few years out of residency, ready to go out and save the world, all while shucking the rigors of his rich, privileged life—never mind that his rich, privileged life was what had enabled him to graduate from medical school without the crippling debt that some of his colleagues had. Now he was nearing forty—thirty-eight, if he was being exact—and he'd spent a long time chasing some utopian dream, only to find that it didn't exist.

No matter how far he ran, he was still himself.

And now, wasn't that a melancholy thought for so early in the morning?

Cool.

Sighing, he tossed his bag onto the passenger's seat and got into his hybrid. The car still smelled new, and it was. Another purchase from his trust fund, another ding against his conscience.

And yet, he'd needed a way to get to and from work.

So once again, convenience had given way to holding the line of his ethics.

Add self-disgust to the melancholy for a lovely mix of morning emotions.

"Fuck," he muttered, turning on his car and backing out of the spot. "I need to get some sleep."

Sleep away the memories. Sleep away the urge to go back. Sleep away everything but the work.

FIVE

Trix

SHE WAS face down in bed when her phone rang.

"Why?" she groaned, fingers fumbling on her nightstand as she tried to grab her cell. It buzzed out of her grip several times before she forced her head up, used her eyes to locate and her hand to grab it, then collapsed back onto her pillow and brought it to her ear.

Where it rang again.

"Fuck," Trix muttered, flopping over to her back, swiping her finger across the screen, and then bringing it up to her ear again. "'lo?" she grumbled.

"Trixie," Heather said brightly. "How's work going?"

That was both way too much cheer and way too much volume for this early in the morning.

She grunted in reply.

Which was a mistake. She should have sat up, blinked away the sleep, and reassured Heather everything was going fine. But instead, all Trix did was pique her sister's mother hen tendencies.

Her sister was recently married—well, she'd gotten married about two years ago. But now that she was happily hitched to Clay, and even Trix could say he was a good man, Heather was determined to see everyone around her happy.

If only she'd stayed abroad, then she would be safely out of Heather's crosshairs.

But Trixie had wanted to come home.

She'd missed northern California, missed its rolling hills and giant redwoods, missed the beaches and the mountains, missed San Francisco and its restaurants, Napa and its wineries, the little beach towns dotted across the coast.

After nearly a decade of escaping her family, she'd wanted to come home.

Not to her family, she thought with a shudder. But to California.

Heather's voice rose in volume, jarring Trix out of her thoughts. "Did something happen at work? Who do I need to kill?" She laughed. "Or sic Bec on, anyway."

Bec being Rebecca Darden, a famous employment law attorney and one of her sister's best friends. Friends as in plural, as in Heather was part of a group of cackling, intervening, happily paired women who thought nothing of sticking their noses into someone's business.

Into *her* business.

"I'm fine," Trix hurried to say, *now* sitting up and blinking the sleep from her eyes. "We had a couple of people call out sick last night, so I worked some overtime." She yawned. "I only just got home." Overtime both had the purpose of padding her bank account and helping to pass the hours.

So, she hadn't seen too many of those wonderful California features yet.

But she'd planned on it today, or at least driving to the coast and listening to the waves.

After some sleep.

"Want to grab breakfast?" Heather asked. "It's been a couple of weeks since our dinner. Did anything come of you and Jet? I want to know everything. Did he call? No, wait, you should just meet us at Molly's." *Us* being her group of friends, or perhaps, more aptly described, her group of intervening busybodies.

Not that Trix didn't like them. She'd actually hung out with the group a few times since moving back. The girls were funny and sweet but . . . they would also be the first to admit without apology that they'd earned an A+ at the whole intervening busy-body thing.

And Trix didn't want the world to know every bit of her life, including the fact that she knew Jet, that he'd broken her heart three years before, and that they were now working together.

That would either get the matchmaking going, or have Heather truly siccing Bec on someone.

Someone being Jet.

And Trix was done. She'd moved on past the heartbroken, past the pissed and wanting to slash his proverbial tires or bog him down with some sort of legal magic Bec could whip up.

Trix had moved on.

The past was the past.

No use dwelling on it.

"I'm tired," Trix said then because she wasn't a total asshole, added, "I just got off after working twelve hours and have a shift tonight. Can I catch up with you guys another time?"

Even though she and Heather had never seemed to be able to find their stride as sisters, or rather, as *half*-sisters, Heather had always tried to bridge the gap between them, had always managed to find a way to check in with Trix over the years, whether by email or phone call or letter. In fairness, Trix hadn't always been open to the contact, but things had changed, she'd grown and matured. Her sister had weathered that process and so, at the very least, she deserved an explanation.

A pause.

Then Heather's voice was decidedly less chipper. "Sure, Trix. I understand."

Shit. "I would come if I wasn't—"

"Of course," Heather said. "I'll talk to you some other time."

"Heath—"

"Abby wanted me to tell you she said hi."

Trix sucked in a breath. "I say hi back—"

"Great, bye."

Click.

The call cut off.

Her guilt was a familiar feeling, but what Heather didn't understand was that Trix was trying, too. Yes, she'd moved home because she loved the towns and the beaches and the mountains and trees, but she could find those same features elsewhere. Part of the reason she'd moved home was also because her family was here. No, because *Heather* was here. Heather being the one person biologically related to her that had always tried to keep in touch.

Maybe she didn't know how to express that desire, but she was there, wasn't she?

That should count for something.

Trix dropped back to the pillows. "I *should* get points for trying," she grumbled. "Especially after working twelve hours straight."

Exhaustion weighed her limbs, made her lazy. She tucked the covers up to her chin and let her lids slide closed. But sleep wouldn't come. Aside from the well-familiar feeling of guilt she had in regards to Heather, the call had woken her brain enough that no matter how long she lay there with her eyes closed, cuddling into a pillow that was infinitely softer than any she'd used over the last decade, cool cotton sheets draped over her body, soft hum of the ceiling fan spinning . . . none of those creature comforts could lure her back under.

After an hour, she tossed back the covers and moved to the bathroom.

Since sleep wasn't an option, she was going to find comfort at the beach.

WAVES WERE LOUD.

At least those of the Pacific Ocean variety.

But at least the noise of the water pounding against the shore had quieted the cacophony in her mind.

Part of her felt like she should have bypassed the beach and gone to meet her sister. Another piece thought that was too much too soon. Another . . . well she was trying not to think about her life.

Or Jet.

Or the fact she'd seen him almost every day she'd been at the hospital, short bursts of viewing as he'd come on and she'd left, a delicate floating note of his scent coating the air and sending a sharp pain through her heart.

Memories, such sweet, fucking memories.

Snorting, she pushed up from where she'd sat down on the sand, gathering up her flip-flops along with the paperback she hadn't ended up reading because she'd been too focused on the glimpses of the sky on the horizon, on the white caps dotting the blue waves, the curls of fog being blown to shore by a wind that tangled her ponytail and chilled the exposed skin on her face and neck.

It was summer in the city.

And summer often began with fog.

But that fog was burning off now, and it was going to be a beautiful day. Soon the beach was going to be crowded with couples and families, with kids off from school, instead of joggers and the occasional person walking their dog. They'd run in the waves, build sandcastles, dig giant holes.

Or maybe that was what she wished she'd been able to do when she was their age.

And *that* was a mental train she wasn't going down.

She would rather wax poetic about how good Jet had been in bed than think about the clusterfuck that had been her childhood.

Suffice it to say, it hadn't included trips to the beach.

It had barely included food in the pantry, never mind a ride to school. However, it *had* included plenty of red-bottomed shoes, plenty of purses and clothes, plenty of makeup.

All essentials according to her mom.

All things that did not grow a healthy child.

But that was the past. She was over it. She was fine now.

Or, if not *fine,* then at least she was at least functional.

And based on her upbringing, that was probably as much as she could ever hope for.

SIX

Jet

IT HAD BEEN two weeks since he'd first seen Trix at the hospital, and they'd crossed paths exactly seven times, mostly him coming in as she was leaving, but one time they'd brushed arms over the coffee cart in the cafeteria.

Brushed arms.

Next, he'd be talking about how the brief contact had made goose bumps rise on his arms.

For the record, it had.

Yes, he was losing his mind.

But tonight he'd come in and Trix was still working, black smudges of fatigue beneath her eyes, hair pulled back into a sloppy ponytail with small, curling tendrils escaping to dip across her forehead. He'd seen her eyes like that too many times to count over the years, knew she'd been picking up any and all overtime she could grab.

And that pissed him off.

They weren't in the field. She shouldn't be working herself to exhaustion instead of enjoying her life. Even though he'd called it quits on their relationship, it wasn't like he didn't care for her.

He'd wanted it to work between them. He tried and, in the end, he'd known it couldn't work, that they both needed more —*him* someone who was open, who could love him without reserve, *her* someone who could peel away the layers, make the effort to love the woman he knew she was underneath. He couldn't do that, not after spending so much of his life pathetically desperate and begging, urging and coaxing for just an iota of love from his parents.

Jet couldn't be like that again.

Not ever again.

But it also didn't mean that he wanted to see a woman he thought of fondly working herself to death.

She'd disappeared into a patient room by the time he walked to the computer and checked the charts then picked up his phone for the shift—so nurses and admins could reach him easily. Since the patient was one he'd need to see anyway, Jet headed into the room.

Trix was removing a blood pressure cuff from the man's arm as he walked in. She glanced up, freezing for one brief moment before her eyes darted away and she removed the thermometer from beneath the patient's tongue. One spin and she turned to the trash can where a flick of her fingers dropped the liner of the thermometer into the trash. Her next sharp movement gave him her back as she began to log the stats into the computer.

"This is Tom," she said. "His BP is 143 over 86. Temp is normal. Came in with chest pain. No prior cardiac episodes or history of heart issues."

Jet nodded his thanks and started to unwind his stethoscope. "Hi, Tom, I'm Dr. Hansen. Is it all right if I take a look at you and ask you a few questions?"

The chart told him Tom was sixty-four, but he looked good

for that age. Not overweight, good coloring, though he was a little pale. Still, chest pain was never something to discount.

Tom nodded. "Sure. Thanks, doc."

Jet began his rundown, listening to his lungs and heart, asking about his pain level—a seven—and what kind of pain Tom was feeling—squeezing. Neither of those made Jet think this was less concerning, so he ordered an EKG, blood tests, and asked Trix to start an IV and administer aspirin and saline, since Tom appeared a bit dehydrated.

"We'll get you taken care of, okay?" Jet told him, putting the stethoscope back around his neck and resting his hand on Tom's arm. "I'm going to go push those tests through so we can have some answers."

Tom nodded. "Thanks."

Jet left the room, heading back to the computers, getting the phlebotomist the orders, making sure the EKG happened as soon as possible.

By the time he finished with that, Trix had come out of the room, brushing a hand across her forehead. Even from ten feet away, he could see that it shook and that made fury crawl up his spine. He crossed to her, snagging her arm and pulling her down the hall. "What the fuck do you think you're doing?"

Stormy gray eyes blinked up at him. "What are you talking about, Dr. Hansen?"

"Jet," he gritted out. "And I'm talking about you."

"You gave up your right to talk about me three years ago." She jerked at his hold, snapping out, "Let go of me."

He dropped his hand but didn't back away. Partly because he was pissed she wasn't taking care of herself again, that she was clearly exhausted and working extra hours that she didn't need to take on. Partly, because she would keep pushing herself through this since some fucked up part of her thought that *this*— being a nurse, taking care of others—was her only worth.

She couldn't see, wouldn't *ever* see that she was so much more.

Jet sighed. "You're exhausted."

Her teeth clicked together. "I'm fine."

Fury faded, bleakness taking its place. "Still the same," he said. "Still can't see—" His phone rang, and he pulled it out of his pocket, glancing at the ID. "Do what you want, Trix. Work yourself ragged to the detriment of everything else in your life." He turned, started to walk away. "It's what you do best."

The phone rang again, but this time he answered it.

There wasn't any point in *not* answering it.

Trix didn't stop him from walking away this time, just as she didn't stop him from walking away then.

HE AND TRIX stayed far apart for the rest of the shift, aside from coordinating Tom's care. The EKG showed he was having a heart attack, and so he was quickly admitted and brought to the Cath Lab where he would have a catheter inserted and his arteries cleaned out.

His prognosis was good, however. He'd come to the ED quickly, had received rapid care. He was in good shape and healthy, and so likely would be heading home after a short time in the ICU.

Trix and Jet were in less than good shape.

They'd barely spoken a word to each other over the course of twelve hours, and now they found themselves both in the break room at the same time, all of four stalls apart as they gathered their stuff from their respective lockers.

With a heavy sigh, Trix slammed the locker door and turned to face him. "I don't need you to take care of me, you know that, right?"

Jet gritted his teeth, grabbing his cell from the locker and shoving it into his pocket.

"In fact," she said and crossed her arms over her chest. "It's probably best for our working arrangement if you *don't* interject yourself in my life."

"I'm not trying to interject myself—"

She sniffed. "Could have fooled me."

"I've worked with you enough to know when you're exhausted," he said, crossing his own arms. "And you're dragging ass, Trix."

"I'm fine," she said through clenched teeth.

Jet blew out a breath. "You're running on fumes. I know it. You know it. You just don't want to admit it because you're fucking stubborn."

Trix rolled her eyes, giving him her back as she shouldered her bag then strode to the fridge and grabbed her lunchbox. "Well, it's a good thing we're not fucking anymore because you don't have to give two shits about me or my *stubbornness*."

Red was creeping into the edges of his vision. "I care about you, Trix," he growled. "You know I do."

"Pft." She headed for the door. "Why now, Jet? Huh? You're so desperate for someone to fuck that I'm suddenly on the menu again?"

He slammed his locker, intercepted her. "That's not fair."

"Well, you said 'fuck' to fair years ago," she snapped. "Why change now?"

Calm.

Calm.

He could manage a full ED with a short staff, could oversee a clinic without fresh water or electricity without breaking a sweat, but Trixie could make him madder than a toddler who'd had his lollipop stolen. She'd always been able to make him feel way too much.

"How was I not fair, Trix?" he said, coming closer, near enough to see the hint of blue in her eyes, to smell that tropical scent of her.

Her lids shut for a heartbeat, her shoulders lifting and falling on a long breath.

Jet felt a pulse of guilt. She'd worked two shifts. He knew she was exhausted, and now he was arguing with her. He should just let her go home and—

Those lids peeled back, and the pain in her gray eyes hit him in the gut.

"You left, Jet," she said. "I gave you more than any other person, and you *fucking left*."

The slice from her words was almost visceral, but the impact to his heart from witnessing the hurt in her expression as she spoke was definitely palpable. He didn't think, didn't bother with words.

He reached for her.

But she was already backing up, batting his hands away.

"Trix," he murmured.

"Don't," she said. "Just leave it, Jet. Just leave the past where it belongs."

She grabbed for the door handle, yanked it open, then ran out of the room.

This time it was *him* watching *her* go.

Unsurprisingly, this version of the scenario didn't feel good either.

And it felt even worse when she didn't come back to the hospital.

SEVEN

Trix

OH GOD, oh God, oh God.

Why had she said that? Why had—

"Fuck," she muttered, keeping her head down as she hurried to her car. Probably because she was as exhausted as Jet had accused her of being.

It *had* been a long week, all of the extra shifts she'd been racking up having taken their toll on her body, her mind, and clearly on her fucking out of control emotions. Why had she admitted that Jet had hurt her?

"I mean, not that it's not obvious." She sighed, unlocking her car and tossing her stuff inside.

She'd been devastated when Jet had gone.

But, come on, like she'd needed to confirm as much to the man?

Where was all of her the-past-is-the-past bullshit? Or maybe it was exactly that . . . *meaning* it was all bullshit. Her strength, her ability to be content in her life, to not wish for more or to want her life to have been different so she could be the type of woman a man like Jet might want permanently—

Stop.

She slammed her hand on the steering wheel.

"No. Fuck this," she muttered. "I am not this person. I am not this weak. I'm fucking *not.*"

But she wasn't sure who she was trying to convince.

Herself? Jet? The universe?

Some fucked up combination of all three?

All she truly knew was that she was too tired to ferret out the truth.

IT WAS a special sort of hell to be on a girls' trip when she'd worked the number of hours she had in the last week.

Just the sheer volume of conversations alone was hell on her brain.

Trix had slept for twelve hours straight before frantically packing a bag and hustling her ass to Heather's place where a party bus—seriously, a *party bus*—had picked up her and the rest of the cackling busybodies.

Speaking of, they'd laughed hysterically when Trix had called them that upon first entering said bus and being peppered with questions about the blind date with Jet.

Sera had grinned when she'd pulled herself back together. "Yup."

Bec had fist-pumped and declared, "That's right! I'm finally recognized for something other than my law skills."

Heather had shaken her head though her lips were twitching.

Kelsey had nodded.

And then Rachel had shoved a protein bar into Trix's hand,

Abby had tossed her a blanket, and they'd left her alone to doze for the drive.

So the negative side to the term busybody wasn't exactly fair, not when their intervening came from caring. But since they seemed to get a kick out of her declaring it, Trix was going to keep it in her back pocket. She'd need some fodder to dish back the teasing this crew gave.

Trix had agreed to go on the trip in the first place because Heather had asked, but also because Heather's friends were cool and she liked them. She had come home because she wanted to start forming some meaningful relationships, and Heather's group of girlfriends had been super nice and welcoming.

Of course, they were still nosy as hell.

But now Trix understood that it came from a place of love and wanting their friends happy. Which made it perfectly acceptable in Trix's book—caring for other people was kind of her specialty.

She'd be happy to call them friends. She *wanted* to crawl out of her shell enough to be able to count them as friends.

But she felt absolutely raw inside, partly because she was still exhausted from working over twenty-four hours straight and partly because . . . Jet.

What else?

She'd been off-center from the moment she'd turned around in that restaurant last month and seen that six-feet-plus gorgeous male specimen walking toward her. He'd rocked her world, made her long for what she couldn't have, and he'd left.

Again.

Now he was back. Present in her daily life. At work, with her friends and family. She was trying to adjust to her new life, and Jet was already all over it.

"Yo! Wakie wakie!" Bec bellowed, making Trix jump. "We're heeere!"

In fairness, Trix had been dozing off over the last two hours, letting the conversation between Heather and her friends— Abby, Seraphina, Rachel, Bec, CeCe, and Kelsey wash over her.

It was comfortable in some ways, to be surrounded by gabbing women. She didn't know ninety percent of the inside jokes, but she did like the teasing behind it. Light-hearted poking fun, lots of laughter, embarrassing stories about Heather and her inability to hold tequila.

It had been nice to just sit back and listen.

She sat up and stretched her neck from side to side, finding the party bus—good lord—had, in fact, stopped. The other girls were lifting bags and hauling them onto their shoulders. All except Sera, who was arguing with Abby about carrying her bag.

"You're like a hundred months pregnant," Abby said, reaching for the bulging duffle.

Sera, a tall, statuesque blonde who easily could be a model, even in her one-hundred-months pregnant state, stepped to the side and blocked Abby.

Abby, Bec, and Sera had been friends well before Heather met Abby when she was interviewing Abby for a job at Robo-Tech. Abby was married to Heather's brother and had spent several hundred months pregnant herself while popping out kiddos left and right. Bec didn't have any kids yet, but based on the conversation on the bus, it wasn't because her husband or Bec didn't want them, rather that Bec was just trying to clear some of her caseload so she'd be able to have some work-life balance.

Either way, Trix knew enough to understand that Sera was thrilled to be pregnant and was blissfully happy with her spouse.

She was also about two seconds away from losing her shit because everyone was treating her as though she were glass.

Trix knew this came from a good place, had heard how Sera had been in a car accident early on in the pregnancy and had experienced some bleeding. But by all of Sera and her doctor's accounts, everything was progressing as it should and she was looking at a normal delivery in about six weeks.

Right in that moment, though, she was in the stabby zone, and so Trix did what she did best.

She intervened.

But smartly.

Slipping past the glaring friends, she bent, grabbed the bag, and walked off the bus.

It took both women some time before they realized what Trix had done, the conversation abruptly cutting off and then footsteps clattering across the floor before Abby and Sera appeared in a huff as they made their way down the stairs.

"Don't you dare," Sera growled when Abby made as though to extend her hand to help her descend the final one.

"Fine," Abby said, hands rising in surrender. "You don't have to be snarly about it."

Since Trix was feeling pretty snarly herself about the fuss Abby was putting on, she thought that Sera exercised an impressive amount of self-control when she came to a rest on the ground, extended her arms to the vineyard surrounding them, and declared, "I need wine!"

Bec snorted. "You got a few more weeks for that."

"You don't even like wine," Abby said.

Sera sniffed. "I don't mind it. You're the heathen who can't stand the stuff."

"I—"

"How about sparkling cider?" Rachel asked. The always-prepared exec at RoboTech pulled out a bottle from her bag.

Sera wrinkled her nose.

"And chocolate?" Rachel added, extracting a chocolate bar with a flourish.

More nose wrinkling, but Sera's eyes were dancing.

"How about we actually go inside the house and get settled?" CeCe said.

"Good plan." Kelsey moved to the lockbox of the AirBnB they'd rented and plugged in the code, extracting a set of keys.

Bec snagged them from her and opened the door, stepping back and declaring, "Preggos get to enter first!"

Sera huffed. "You guys are the worst."

"Accept the offer graciously," Abby called.

Sera whipped around and glared. "Sometimes I wonder why—"

"First in, means you get first choice of the bedrooms," Trix said.

Sera paused on the threshold, eyes meeting Trix's. "Good point." She addressed the group at large. "And I also think that being a hundred months pregnant means that I get to *assign* rooms." She strode into the house, tossing back over her shoulder, "And I declare that Abby is going to sleep in the bus."

"Hey—"

Their driver chose that moment to get back onto the bus. "Well, it's been a pleasure, ladies," he said and shut the door with a *snick*.

Abby looked from the bus, slowly backing down the driveway to the house, eyes wide.

They all burst into laughter.

Even one-hundred-months-pregnant Sera.

Then they carted their butts inside and got some wine. Well, except for Sera. She had sparkling cider.

And chocolate. Couldn't forget the chocolate.

It was two in the morning.

She couldn't sleep.

Probably because she'd basically slept the day away and then dozed on the bus.

But this wasn't a bad place to be stuck *not* sleeping.

Vineyards rolled over the surrounding hills, darkened shadows at this hour, their leaves barely distinguishable in the moonlight. She knew their branches would be heavy with grapes at this time of the year, though they were not ready yet for harvest.

Sighing, she brought her glass to her lips and took a sip of the Zinfandel, the sweetness of the rosé dancing across her tongue. Her father's winery produced a very similar variety, though thankfully none of Heather's friends were the type of people to support a total asshole.

Probably, because their own parents weren't much better.

There was something about money that changed people, turned them into . . . something selfish? Something self-absorbed. Something—

Well, that wasn't fair, was it?

She'd met plenty of selfish and self-absorbed people during her travels, knew those weren't necessarily traits that were isolated to the wealthy.

Maybe it was less that the rich were bigger assholes and more that the wealthy were able to facilitate their needs because they had the funds and power to do so.

She took another sip and set her glass down, reclining back on the chaise that was on the back porch of the house they were staying at.

It was a beautiful find, a one-story ranch with eight bedrooms and ten bathrooms—yes, she'd counted, yes, she'd also got the full real estate rundown from Sera on the way in. Apparently, Sera had tried to get her husband to buy the home when they'd first met and had fallen in love. Tate had waffled, someone else had bought it, and now she had to live here vicariously for one weekend.

But the house was set on a smaller vineyard, a hobby-type one that was more for show than production. Unlike her father's, which was somewhere over the hills, acres and acres of wine-grade grapes filling the vines, an army of workers tending the grapes, aiding with production, hosting tastings.

It was a lucrative business.

And yet, it was as important to her father as this hobby farm was to the owner of this house.

As in, it wasn't important at all.

Her father had made his money in tech and military contracts, but everything else he had his fingers in—wine, a cruise line, a professional hockey team based out of L.A., an airline—was just a hobby.

A billion-dollar set of hobbies.

Insanity.

And yet, no tuition for medical school. No donation to the medical organization she'd worked with when they'd been critically short of supplies after a hurricane in the Caribbean. Heather and Jordan had donated. Abby and Sera had donated. Bec had donated. Tanner, her friend, not yet having "made" it had donated even though he'd been struggling at the time. Trix also knew that even though she'd just met Kelsey, Rachel, and CeCe that they too would have opened their wallets.

But her dad. Nope. Her mom. Definitely not. She lived from alimony payment to alimony payment and, as a consequence, could rarely rustle up money for "extra" things.

Let it be noted that those extra things often included items like food. Or paying the electricity bill. Hell, until Trix had moved halfway around the globe, she'd received many a call from her mom wondering why the lights didn't work.

Ridiculous.

A grown woman with four children, who should have been set for life, who should have been able to take care of them easily, had just bailed on any and all responsibility.

It was no wonder that Bobby, Will, and Kevin had turned out the way they were.

Namely, assholes.

But they'd learned from the best.

And everyone coped in their own way.

She just . . . wished that things had been different. That her parents had gotten their shit together and actually acted like parents, that she could find a way to connect with her siblings, including pushing through the reserve with Heather, who didn't deserve her tentativeness. Trix should be able to connect with the one person in her life who'd been steady and there. She should be able to open herself up to the fact that Heather's wonderful group of friends was fine with including her and not making her feel like she was an obligation or something to be tolerated.

But . . . how to push through or be open?

It was absolutely terrifying.

She didn't stay and fight for things she wanted—didn't demand her dad pay for school or her mother get her shit together, didn't pressure Jet to stay or declare his unending love. That just wasn't the way she operated. Trix managed it herself and if for some godawful reason she *had* to ask and was turned down, she simply adjusted her expectations and surrounded herself with a safety net. That net kept toxic people out, kept her heart and mind and soul safe and . . .

Maybe it wasn't the healthiest, but she purposefully created distance between herself and all of the bad in the world.

From the disappointment, the heartache, the betrayals.

The being left behind, forgotten.

But after spending the evening with her sister's friends, after being wrapped up in conversation and included and laughed with, Trix had to wonder if the net that kept her safe was also hurting her.

Was the anxious feeling she'd been experiencing her mind revolting?

Telling her she'd been alone for too long?

That the net was harming her more than it protected?

Because if she was always behind that net, always hiding and safely ensconced from the world, then how could she ever be free?

So many questions. So unsettled.

Still, so alone.

Sighing, she picked up her glass, tilted her gaze to the stars, and kept drinking.

She wouldn't find the answers tonight.

But perhaps this was the first step to finding them eventually.

EIGHT

Jet

HE SPENT two days freaking out about Trixie not showing up for work before he broke down and by the third asked the charge nurse when she was scheduled again.

He'd made an excuse about wanting to follow up with Trix about their patient, Tom, and his prognosis, but Rosario didn't look like she believed him, and anyway, it wasn't like Trixie needed him to tell her about the patients when she could follow up about them herself.

Still, he'd probably looked like a moron, but he had found out that Trix's absence was planned.

Two additional days off, plus her normal three.

Like most of the other nurses in the area, she worked four tens on and then had three days off, while the docs in the department worked three twelve-hour shifts a week.

Regardless, Rosario had given him an assessing look and then told him that she'd be back on Wednesday. Wonderful. He was off until Thursday.

Which meant he'd been an ass and had to wait almost a week to apologize.

What was it that people said about doctors and egos? That they had them in the plenty and that they also weren't small. *Kind of like something else*, he thought and snorted at his lame high school joke as he gathered his stuff and took off for home.

He had a couple of days off before his next shift on Thursday, might as well make the most of them.

First, sleep.

Second, getting some furniture because his place was seriously lacking. He was thirty-eight and that meant he shouldn't be living off an air mattress with a wall-mount TV propped in one corner.

He needed a real mattress, a bed frame, maybe a couch, and a dining room table. Hell, he could even spring for some chairs.

Living the big life.

Ha.

His cell rang as he took his exit from the freeway. He glanced at the caller ID and saw that Clay was calling.

"Hey, man," he answered over Bluetooth.

"Hey." A beat before his friend's voice continued through the speakers. "I'm bored."

Jet was stunned into silence for a long moment. Probably because he'd never *ever* heard Clay say he was bored. Never. Clay Steele was a workaholic in the most classic sense of the world. They'd met when he, Heather, and Colin McGregor pooled resources and wanted to test using their artificial intelligence to get medical supplies and food to areas hit hard by natural disasters. Places where limited crews and shipments could get in, but where the need was intense.

Clay had unending energy, worked hours that compared with Jet's, and he always had about ten projects fired up and waiting on the back burner.

It was unfathomable that Clay could be bored.

Also unfathomable?

The pathetic tone of Clay's voice.

He sounded despondent, almost pouty.

"Heather take over all your work?" Jet asked.

Clay sighed. "No," he grumbled. "She extended her trip by a day, and now I'm home alone with no work because Sebastian won't let me take over his projects."

Jet laughed. "This is what happens when you hire people who are too good at what they do."

"That's what I'm saying," Clay muttered.

"How long has Heather been gone?"

"Since Friday, she and the girls went on a long weekend up to Sonoma," Clay said. "Now they're not coming back until tomorrow. Apparently, Trix found some sort of hot spring spa they want to try, so they extended their rental."

Jet's heart skipped a beat at the mention of Trix's name, and he deliberately ignored the pulse of alarm that trailed it. Probably because his dumb ass mouth was working. "Trix is with them?"

Clay grunted. "Eight women in that house. Drinking, watching marathons of *Magic Mike* and *Aquaman* and *Thor*, getting into trouble and—"

"Dude," Jet interrupted, navigating the stop-and-go that always crowded the last few blocks before his building. "You need to chill out. Order a pizza, grab a beer, and relax. Your girl will be home in twenty-four hours."

"I haven't seen her for four days."

Jet rolled his eyes. "Also, this just in, you're completely pussy-whipped."

"So what," Clay muttered.

"*So*, you should be okay being without Heather for a few days."

"I'm *okay*," Clay said. "I just don't like it."

"And you're apparently worried she's going to leave you for a stripper? Or a superhero?"

A long-suffering sigh. "No."

"Then relax. Enjoy being able to put your feet up on the table without getting yelled at. Have that beer, order that pizza."

"It's eight in the morning."

"Okay, wait a few hours *then* do both."

"Fine," Clay said, tone still grumbling. "Be reasonable, why don't you?"

"I will," Jet agreed. "Other than missing your wife, what have you been up to?"

They shot the shit as Jet pulled into the underground parking garage and made his way up to his condo, Clay telling him about some projects that were rolling out, including some cool innovations with AI that hospitals might be able to use shortly.

"You working today?" Clay asked as Jet walked into his condo.

"Just got off shift. Not working again until Thursday."

"Cool. Then you can order the pizza tonight. I'll bring the beer over to your place."

Jet dropped his stuff by the door. "Fair warning. My plan is to buy a couch today, but my furniture situation is a little sparse."

"Do you have a TV?"

"Yeah."

"Good enough for me." A beat then, "Should we bother with vegetables on the pizza?"

Jet kicked off his shoes, dropped onto the air mattress. "Nah."

Clay laughed. "Agree," he said. "Okay, I'm going to have my assistant send you some places that can have furniture delivered." There was a pause, as though Clay were glancing at the time. "I'm guessing you're going to crash now?"

Jet's eyes were already closed. "You'd be guessing right."

"Cool, I'll have Tristan email you the places."

"Not billionaire places," Jet said.

"Not billionaire," Clay agreed. "See you about eight tonight."

"'kay."

They hung up. Jet blearily managed to plug his cell into the charger and then tugged the covers up and over him.

He was asleep in seconds.

THE SUN WAS BLINDING when he woke, and Jet spent a few minutes mentally grumbling that he hadn't thought to shut the curtains. Realistically, it was probably a good thing since he probably would have slept until Clay came over and then they'd be sitting on the floor, a pizza box and beers between them, watching a TV that was propped against the wall in one corner of his condo.

That, at least, was enough to get him out of bed. Well, that and the sun shining directly in his eyes.

He crossed to the bathroom, showered quickly, and then got dressed.

As promised, an email from Tristan@steeletechnologies.com was waiting in his inbox, containing a list of furniture stores, along with their styles, their inventory that was able to be shipped that day, and their location relative to his condo.

Tristan was scarily efficient.

Then again, after having recently met Sebastian—Clay's former assistant who had moved up in the company and trained Tristan—his friend didn't seem to accept them any other way.

Furniture shopping.

Yay.

Every grown man's dream.

Snorting, he tucked his cell in his pocket, grabbed a jacket, and got down to furnishing his condo.

Thankfully, the process wasn't too painful, and after a couple of hours Jet had a couch being delivered later that day, a bed frame and new mattress coming the next, and had filled his cart at Target to an obscene amount with new sheets and blankets, towels, pillows, and an area rug.

Even a man who'd spent more of the last few years in tents and sleeping on the ground, at worst, or an air mattress, at best, could be tamed by a walk through the home goods aisle at Target.

Now he was home, had mounted the TV to the wall, unpacked most of the bags, thrown the new sheets in the wash, and was moving his limited furniture to the side to make room for the kick-ass sectional he'd picked out. If Jet was becoming domesticated, he figured he might as well be comfortable at the same time, and so the pieces he'd chosen were solid and comfortable *and* had taken a giant chunk out of his paycheck.

Worth it, though.

If he was serious about wanting to settle down and have a family, he'd need furniture.

And it wasn't like he was going to be bringing a woman back to his place to get busy on an air mattress.

Come home with me, baby. I'll try not to fuck you hard enough to deflate the bed.

Yeah, that would be super smooth.

The buzzer rang, and his next hour was spent helping the guys bring the furniture in and then logging into all of his streaming accounts on the TV. Clay arrived with beer and the pizza in hand—having intercepted the guy in the hall, and they turned on a baseball game while making a respectable dent in the six-pack and extra-large pizza.

It was probably the most normal night he'd had in six years.

A friend, a game, some food, plenty of shit-talking.

"How'd it go with Trix?" Clay asked as they were carrying the empties into the kitchen.

"We going to have heart-to-hearts now?" Jet countered.

"Well, we already discussed in length how I'm severely pussy whipped," Clay said. "The least you can do is tell me my matchmaking efforts were successful."

Jet rolled his eyes. "Seriously?"

"Come on, man. She's perfect for you. She's smart, not interested in that giant wad of money your parents left you, and bonus, absolutely gorgeous."

Those were all true statements. Ones he knew, of course, being that he'd spent almost a year of his life learning everything he could about Trix—everything she'd allowed him to know, that was. The trouble was, Clay didn't know about that year. In fact, he doubted *anyone* did. Not only had their work often separated them, taking them on different assignments to different parts of the world, but during the times they were together, they'd needed to be discreet—not only because it was against policy to fraternize, but because some of the places they'd been were culturally different and they wouldn't have appreciated an unwed couple with a standing evening sex appointment to be administering their care.

It had been tricky.

It had been exciting.

He'd fallen deep and he'd fallen fast.

But Clay didn't know any of that.

And Jet wasn't willing to share it with the class.

"She's a nurse, Jet," Clay added when he didn't say anything. "She's traveled. She did the whole doctoring abroad thing like you, but for even longer. Heather hardly saw her for a full decade before she moved back home."

Jet knew all of that. Well, not the not seeing her sister part, though he supposed that wasn't too much of a surprise considering how all-encompassing that world had been. When they were on an assignment, it was hard to think of anything but what was right in front of them. Not only was it tough and exhausting, but oftentimes they weren't near any place where they *could* call home, even if they'd had the physical or mental energy to do so. But he knew the rest of it, that she'd lived abroad from almost the moment she'd graduated from nursing school, that she was brilliant and talented and could suture a wound better than he could.

He knew she could have been a doctor, would have probably been a better one than he was.

She was just that good.

But she'd barely been able to afford to put herself through nursing school.

Somehow despite being the daughter of George O'Keith, money had been tight. Jet didn't know the story as to why, whether O'Keith had refused to pay, or whether *she'd* refused, not wanting to be tied down. Yet, that probably as much as anything else, illustrated exactly why he and Trix couldn't work out.

A year together and he hadn't begun to understand her relationship with her family.

He shoved the pizza box into the trash and turned to face Clay. "She works at the hospital."

Clay's brows rose. "Which hospital?"

"*My* hospital," he said. "In the same department. It's too messy, even if she was interested in me. Which she's not."

"Did you even call her?"

Jet started sticking the empty beer bottles into the recycling can. "I saw her *at the hospital*."

Clay rubbed his chin, the bristle on his jaw making a loud scratching sound. "That is dicey. You guys work at the same time?"

He nodded. "Sometimes."

"Hmm." Clay shrugged. "Well, Heather's going to be disappointed. She wants everyone around her happy and paired off."

Jet straightened. "*I* want to be happy and paired off, but as much as I like Trix, I'm not going to pursue something that puts both of our jobs at risk."

"Sometimes things work out better when you work together."

"That's easy to say when you're the boss," Jet said. "Meanwhile, I don't think *my* boss would be so happy about that scenario."

Clay grinned. "That's a fair point." He turned and grabbed his jacket off the back of the couch—which, note to the universe was really fucking comfortable. "You know what the solution to this is, right?"

Jet trailed him to the door. "What?"

"You become the boss, and then you get to do what you want."

Jet snorted. "So says the man with the giant HR Department."

Clay winced, hand on the knob. "It is obscenely large."

Jet paused, lips twitching. "Almost forty, and still so tempted to make a *that's what she said* joke."

Clay snorted. "Never too old for bad jokes."

"True." They shook hands. "Next time you need to forget you're missing your wife, I'm around."

"I'll take you up on that," Clay said. "Also, know that now

you're on Heather's and the rest of the Sextant's radar. So get ready for matchmaking efforts galore."

"What's a Sextant?"

Clay waved a hand. "It's a long story that involves an obscene amount of drunk Googling and a gaggle of women. The point is, Heather's got a good circle of friends, but they're all paired off. Now, they're looking for fresh meat."

Jet chuckled. "Well, consider me fresh meat then. If they have anyone as cool as Heather, I'd be all over that."

His eyes narrowed. "She's mine."

"That I'm well aware, my friend," Jet said. "My point was that you have good taste."

Clay grinned. "That I do."

"So, if there's another Heather around. One that's not yours," he added when Clay started scowling again. "Then, I'm in."

With a nod, Clay headed toward the elevator. "Just saying, there *is* another Heather around."

"Yeah?"

Clay pressed the button to call the car and glanced back over his shoulder. "Yeah. Her name is Trix."

NINE

Trix

SHE'D HAD fun with the girls, more fun than she would have expected, especially on their final day together, when they'd all blown off responsibility and had gone to the hot springs she'd nervously suggested the previous day in Calistoga.

They hadn't shot her down.

They'd actually extended their trip by a day and had all gone with her.

Trix grinned. So yeah, she had friends now.

Still, despite having grown up in the Bay Area, she had never done a lot of the touristy stuff. No cable car, no Alcatraz, no Hearst Castle or Missions.

When she'd bought her first car, she'd put as much gas in the tank as she could afford and then had driven wherever the tank would get her. To the beach, to Pier 39, to Tahoe once or twice when she'd really gotten good tips at work. But it had never taken her to Calistoga or Lassen or Death Valley. She'd never made it down to San Diego or even to Yosemite.

Trix had been all around the world and yet, had hardly explored her home state.

Well, that was going to change now.

First with Calistoga, and to be able to check it off her list felt good. Next week, she was going to do a tour of Alcatraz.

Feeling proud of herself both for surviving the weekend—because yes, the other women were great and fun and had included her in everything, but they were also a lot for a woman who wasn't used to that much socialization—but she was also proud for actually having a plan to live her life more fully.

For the first time ever she had goals and hopes and dreams, and she wasn't going to compromise them.

So, yes, Alcatraz and then Lassen and Death Valley and San Diego. Hell, maybe she'd live vicariously and take a drive down Highway 1.

Go her.

But for now, she had to go to work. The sightseeing and hopes and dreams would have to wait until her next few days off. She was on days from seven in the morning until five at night for the foreseeable future.

Which was a good thing, considering Jet worked nights.

If they had to work at the same place, at least they were on opposing shifts.

See? Look at her go with the bright side. She filled her coffee mug, shrugged into her backpack, and made her way down to her car. It would feel good to be on her feet for her shift, to walk off all that wine and cheese and lazing around she'd done all weekend.

Plus, Jet wouldn't be there.

She could work and focus on her job and not have to worry about betraying something to the man who'd broken her heart.

The one she'd declared that she cared about just a few days before.

"Ugh," she groaned, starting up her car, having almost forgotten that critically embarrassing moment.

Well, she had twenty-four more hours to get over it because Jet didn't work Wednesdays . . . and *go her* for having the where-withal to have checked the schedule before she left.

The drive was its typical stop-and-go, but inching her way to the hospital at least let her get caught up on her podcasts.

That day's presentation was about a guy who let snakes bite him to build up his tolerance to venom, a la *The Princess Bride* and the Iocane powder Battle of the Wits, though no one had died.

Yet.

The nurse in her shook her head.

The woman who'd become obsessed with reality TV of late was fascinated.

But by the time she'd pulled into the parking lot, Trix had moved on to music and she was softly singing a song by Rhianna as she got out of her car and gathered her stuff.

"Always did have a pretty voice."

She jumped, narrowly avoiding banging her head on the frame of the car, and whipped around to glare at Jet.

"What the fuck?" she snapped. "You like sneaking up on women?"

A quick flash of white. "I never could resist doing it to you."

She rolled her eyes, tossed her backpack over one shoulder, then closed the door and locked her car. "I thought you weren't working today."

The moment the words were out of her mouth, she knew she'd made a mistake.

Trix had just all but told Jet she'd been aware enough of him to know his schedule. Paired with the whole *I-care-about-you* nonsense and—

Run.

As in, she needed to get the hell out of there.

"Well, good to see you," she said hurriedly and took off for the hospital.

He followed her.

Oh, good Lord.

She pointed toward the parking lot. "Shouldn't you go home and get some sleep?"

"Nope."

Her lips pressed into a flat line, irritation weaving through her, but she didn't snap back an answer like she wanted. Instead, she swallowed her retort and kept walking toward the hospital.

And Jet kept walking right alongside her.

Finally, ten feet from the door, she stopped and spun around to face him. "Seriously, Jet. What the fuck are you doing?"

He clipped on his badge, strode by her. "I'm going to work."

She followed him. "But you don't work this shift."

"That's twice you've mentioned my work hours." He leaned down, knowing eyes alighting on hers for a moment. "Keeping track of me?"

Trix sniffed. "Only as much as to know how to steer clear." She brushed by him. "Too bad that didn't work today."

At the doors, Jet reached past her and swiped his badge to open the panel. "I don't mind working with you. You're the best nurse in this place."

"I wouldn't say that too loudly," she muttered, striding through the door in front of him. "You have to work with all the rest of them, remember?"

"I remember."

"And why are you on days?"

"That was always the plan. I was just filling in for Dr. Joyce while she was on maternity leave."

Trix's gut twisted. "Oh."

They walked in silence the rest of the way to the break room, which was the point that she finally realized something. "Why don't you use the physician break room?"

A shrug. "It's a bit . . ." He trailed off.

"Stuffy?" she filled in.

"If stuffy means filled with arrogant assholes, then yes."

She snorted. Their department was pretty good, but Jet's point wasn't inaccurate. There were a lot of egos on the physician side of the ED. "So you decided to slum it with the rest of the staff?"

"I prefer to quote-unquote"—he did air quotes here and instead of being ridiculous or douchy, they made her smile —"slum it with the people doing the real work."

Trix smiled. "Laying it on thick, Hansen."

He lifted a brow, reaching in front of her to hold open the door to the break room. "That's Dr. Hansen to you," he said, tapping his chest self-importantly.

Pausing in the doorway, she stared at him for a long moment.

But then he made a goofy face and danced the slashes of his dark brown brows across his forehead. Between the eyebrow waggling, the banter, and the silly expression, she was reminded of exactly how it used to be between them. She broke out into laughter and he followed suit, still holding the door open. His body was close to hers, close enough his scent inundated her nose, made her thighs clench. Abruptly, her laughter cut off, the heat of him seeping through the thin layers of her scrubs, making her nipples bead against the soft fabric of her bra.

Jet went quiet, eyes flicking down to her chest, and she knew he saw her nipples standing out in sharp relief by the way every muscle in his body went taut, his hands clenching into fists at his sides.

"Trix," he murmured, voice raspy and scraping its way along her skin.

Not in a bad way.

Rather, it set every one of her nerves on high alert, raised goose bumps on her arms, the hairs on the back of her neck.

And his expression?

That was pure heat, threatening to incinerate her from the inside out.

"Baby," he murmured.

She leaned in, close enough that her nipples brushed his chest. He smelled *so* good and she knew he would feel good against her, those slightly roughened hands brushing up and down her arms, mouth dragging across her jaw until his lips found hers with a firm, but confident pressure, the wet heat of his tongue sliding against hers.

Jet bent slightly and she felt the hot, damp air of his breath against her ear. "Trix," he whispered and *fuck* how she wanted to turn her head, to allow his mouth to meet hers, to kiss and hold and *touch* him like she used to.

For him to wind his fingers into her hair, tilt her head, taste her deeply.

For the fingers to slide down and slip beneath the hem of her shirt, to drift across the skin of her stomach, to flutter up to her breasts—

A monitor alarmed and they jumped apart.

"Help!" someone yelled.

A millisecond later, a Code Blue—a patient's heart stopping —was called.

Trix hit her head against the door frame, hard enough to see stars, but that didn't stop her from lurching into the break room and throwing her stuff into her locker. Jet was right behind her, dropping his stuff before they both sprinted out of the room. A man was standing in the hallway, holding a woman who was covered in blood in his arms.

He wavered as Trix closed the distance between them, and she lunged the final few feet and stuck her shoulder beneath the man's, preventing them from crashing to the ground. A second later, Jet was there, grabbing the woman from the man's arms and barking out orders.

Half the department was in with the coding patient, and the rest sprinted out into the hall.

Two gurneys appeared and they hefted the patients onto them, calling out stats and injuries they saw as they rolled them into rooms. She and Jet ended up separated. He stayed with the woman while she got to work on the man with Dr. Harding. Her patient had a large laceration on his scalp, and what appeared to be a knife wound in his abdomen. He passed out in the middle of answering a question about what had happened but had at least told them his name was Ben and he was thirty-two. They kept working, addressing the injuries they could see, packing wounds, applying pressure, while she started an IV and began pushing fluids, stabilizing him enough to get him down to CT.

Trix knew the same was going on next door, and she also knew that somewhere in another room, her coworkers were also addressing the code that had been called, trying to restart the patient's heart while also doing their best to manage the pressing needs of their other patients.

It didn't matter that it was a shift change, that people might technically be off the clock. They banded together, worked efficiently and quickly to treat the patients in front of them.

Later, it would be time to breathe, to change their bloodied scrubs for clean, to splash some water on their faces, to suck in some air, shore up their spines, and go home or continue on with their shift.

In her room, they got the bleeding under control and moved Ben off to a CT.

She took the time to peel off her gloves and poke her head in next door. Jet's patient was awake now, but pale, answering questions as the team worked on her.

Trix moved to the next desk, made sure everything was under control.

Mostly everything was fine, but they were still trying to resuscitate the patient who'd coded, and it was nearing the time where they were going to have to call it.

Damn.

She stifled a sigh, tucked down the sadness. This was the way of life in the ED, in health care. Patients came, the staff did their utmost to help them, and even after they did everything they could . . . sometimes the patient didn't make it.

Trix spent a few minutes clocking in then walking down to the break room and making sure her and Jet's belongings had actually made it into their lockers with locks that were actually locked. Then realized her cell was still in her pocket, and so she disinfected it then stowed that away.

By the time she left the break room and made it back to the nurse's station, Susan was emerging from a patient room. Based on the expression on her face, Trix assumed it was where they'd had the code.

Susan tossed her gloves in the bin and came over.

"You okay?" Trix asked.

Susan nodded. "Yeah. Just sucks. He'd just been discharged yesterday."

"Oh? From where?"

"Here. He'd had a heart attack last week, a couple of stints were put in, but the prognosis was good."

Trix's breath caught.

"Was his name Tom?"

Susan's eyes met hers, and she nodded. "Yeah. Did you work on him last week?"

Trix nodded.

"Sucks."

Another nod. "Yeah, it does."

They stood together in silence for a few moments, knowing exactly what the other person was feeling—sadness because someone was gone, failure because there were always the "what if's," the "should have's," the "could have's," but also disappointment and fury and a teeth-clenching mix of *all* of those.

Because sometimes medicine didn't win.

Sometimes people died.

But as sad as that was, as heartbreaking, they still had a job to do.

Later, they could cry.

Trix sucked in a breath and released it slowly. "What else do we have?"

Susan was quiet for a beat longer then visibly shook herself and began rattling off the remainder of her patients and what needed to happen on Trix's shift. They discussed everything, got sorted, and then Trix made the rounds while Susan went home.

Those rounds, following up on Ben, administering meds, and checking on test results were *all* she focused on.

Otherwise, she'd think of Tom.

Of sweet, funny, kind Tom who'd joked and laughed and been quite wonderful and who was now . . . gone.

No.

Not thinking about that.

Work. She'd focus on the work, hold it in for the next twelve hours.

Then she could allow herself to break down.

It was ten past seven, she'd just finished the shift change, and Trix was absolutely exhausted. Emotionally, physically, mentally, it was one of those days that she felt every minute of those twelve hours of work.

And she had three more days of the same in front of her.

One small miracle was that she had barely seen Jet for the entirety of her shift. He'd been focusing on the female patient, she'd been with Dr. Harding on Ben and then later dealing with the police when they'd come to investigate the car with its engine running in front of the ED, Ben's stab wound, and . . . oh yeah, the trunk filled to the brim with cocaine.

When she regained her sense of dark humor, that story was going to be a good one to tell.

She shrugged on her backpack, gathered the rest of her things, and headed out.

Jet was leaning against her car, arms and ankles crossed.

"Fuck," she muttered, but she was too tired to try and find a way to avoid this conversation. Instead, she kept walking, striding over to the passenger's side door and bleeping the locks. Her backpack went on the floor, alongside her dirty scrubs.

She briefly debated climbing over the console to get into the driver's seat, but that was too cowardly even for her. So this time, she stifled her f-bomb, backed out of the passenger's side, and rounded the hood.

Jet didn't move as she approached.

Fine. Whatever.

She yanked at the handle, trying to open the door, maybe his ass would get pinched in the opening.

A girl could hope.

But since he was heavy and she managed to get it open all of one inch—yes, she was strong no, she couldn't move a behemoth of a man who outweighed her by a hundred pounds all via a small strip of metal—she stopped and glared at him.

He looked down at her with patient eyes. "You heard about Tom?"

The name was a punch to her gut, and she sucked in a breath.

Jet moved, tugging her into his arms. "Yeah, you heard," he murmured into her hair, running his hand up and down her spine. "Are you okay?"

"I'm fine."

But she *wasn't* fine, and he knew it, and so luckily for her, she got to stay in the circle of his arms.

"It reminds you of Amare."

For as much as she tried to keep herself locked down, Jet always seemed to know exactly she was thinking.

"Yeah."

"That was a tough case."

"They're not the same."

Amare most likely would have lived if he'd had access to the U.S. healthcare system. Aside from his heart problems, he'd been otherwise healthy. And like Tom, he'd been funny and kind. He'd also been a great provider, and just a really special soul all around. Everyone in the clinic had loved him.

Everyone had grieved when they'd lost him.

"That doesn't make this any easier."

That much was true.

Jet dropped his arms and, no, she wasn't disappointed that he'd backed away. She couldn't afford to be sad at this point. It was a fact. He didn't stay, wouldn't *ever* stay long term. Still, regardless of the past shading their present interactions, Jet stepped back. Trix kept her eyes on her shoes, sucking in a few slow breaths, listening to his footsteps as he strode away.

That was fine.

He'd been nice about Tom. Friendly.

That was all she could ever hope for.

It would need to be enough.

A car door opened and closed and still she just breathed, eyes on her feet. Okay, good. Enough. She was going to go home and—

Warm fingers laced through hers.

Her gaze flew up, saw Jet had her backpack over his shoulder, the bag of dirties under his arm. "Come on."

"What—"

Before she could finish her question, Trix was in the passenger's seat of his car, her keys plucked from her fingers and her car's locks *bleeped*. Then faster than she would have thought possible, her seat belt was buckled, her stuff stowed in the backseat, and Jet was pulling out of the parking spot.

"Um . . ."

What had just happened?

"I'm sorry I was such an ass last week."

"Um . . ."

Double, *what just happened?* Because Jet was apologizing?

"I should have trusted you to know your own limits," he said. "I was out of line."

"Yes, you were."

He laughed. "Never one to let anyone off the hook."

Ouch. And just like always, Jet was able to cut her to the quick. Heart aching, she stared out the window, watching the red taillights moving past them for a long moment. The past, the present were tangled together, and she didn't realize for several minutes that they weren't heading in the direction of her place until he got off the freeway way to soon.

She needed to take it south for several more miles, not get off in the city.

"Jet—"

His eyes flashed to hers. "I wanted it to work between us. You know that, right?"

She forgot about the exit as irritation flowed over her. "And by wanting to make it work, you *left*? Didn't explain why you were leaving or where you were going or for how long?" Her palm smacked against her thigh. "We had what I thought was this incredible night together, made plans a-and you didn't return my calls, my emails. You just ghosted me and disappeared off the fucking face of the earth."

His jaw clenched. "I had to go to Haiti."

"Without a word?"

"It wasn't like there was an abundance of communication methods after the earthquake."

"You couldn't have left a note?"

"I . . . didn't have time."

She turned, meeting his eyes for long enough that the car behind them got antsy and honked. Jet hit the accelerator.

"You're full of shit," she said. "Whatever happened, you panicked and left."

"It wasn't panic."

"Then, *what* was it?"

"I knew we'd never work."

Trix huffed. "We seemed to work damned well for over a year."

Silence then, "That was before."

Her gut clenched. "Before what?"

He turned into a garage, hitting the clicker hanging on his sunshade, and pulling into a parking spot before he turned to face her. His eyes and tone were serious as he said, "Before I realized that you were never going to give me what I need."

Slice.

His words cut her deeply, gouging tracks through her heart,

her soul. She'd given this man everything that was in her power to give.

And it still wasn't enough.

She clenched her teeth against the burn in her throat, deliberately blinked to keep the tears in her eyes as she met his gaze. He was serious. He didn't get how much it had taken her to open up to him as much as she had. "I gave you more than I've given any other person."

"I think that's a pretty ex—"

"No," she said. "So maybe I didn't tell you about my parents and their pissing contest with money or how I had to fend for myself because my mother was too wrapped up in clothes and shoes and makeup to buy fucking food." Her breath was slow and controlled. "I tried very hard for *many* years to forget that. But I did tell you how there wasn't a lot of money growing up. I told you I'd dreamed of being a doctor, but had to give up on that and become a nurse instead." She reached into the backseat and snatched her backpack, but she couldn't reach the bag of dirty clothes. Fuck it, Jet could wash them if he really gave a shit. "I gave you . . . *so fucking much*," she snapped. "I gave you everything I could—"

He slammed his hand on the steering wheel. "But you didn't give me any of the why! You didn't tell me why you gave up on the dream, why your brothers left, why you had to fend for yourself. And you sure as shit didn't tell me what you felt about *any* of that."

"I—" She shook her head. "I'm not easy with feelings," she admitted. "I spent so much of my life shoving them down that *I'm* not even sure what I feel most of the time."

His eyes went sad. "And that right there."

She reached for the door handle. "What right there?"

"That," he repeated. "You don't know your own feelings

enough to discuss them like a rational human," he said. "You're not whole, Trix. Your past has cut you to shreds."

More slicing, more hurt tap-dancing on her heart.

"And what? I'm damaged?" she spat. "You didn't have the energy to heal me?"

Jet didn't deny that. Didn't say anything except, "I'm a healer of the body, baby. Not of the mind."

Ah. So that was it. The truth about why he'd left.

She was so incredibly fucked up that she wasn't worth the time and effort to learn what was beneath her armor.

She'd known that. Some part of her had understood. Hell, she was well familiar with her abilities to keep people at a distance. But . . . she hadn't kept Jet away, or hadn't meant to anyway, and that he didn't find value in how much effort it had taken her to give him all she had, to push herself out of her comfort zone as much as she had . . . well, that hurt almost as much as him declaring her damaged.

"Maybe my childhood fucked me up," she said.

"There's no maybe about it."

Anger hazed the edges of her vision. "Okay, so it *clearly* fucked me up," she gritted. "But you're just as fucked up, just as damaged. Maybe I wasn't open, maybe I had too much armor, but you're just as protected, Jet. You didn't even fight for us, didn't express what you needed from me, didn't bother to tell me that you had to have more in order for things to work out." She popped the door handle and started to push out, pausing to toss over her shoulder, "And the reason you didn't do *any* of those things was because you were scared. Scared shitless that what was between us might actually work out, scared *you'd* have to put yourself out there."

"That's—"

"Not fair?" she asked, stepping out and bending to glare at him through the opening. "What's *not* fair is you being in disbelief about the fact that *you're* damaged, too, that your childhood fucked you up just as much, that you're just as good at keeping people at a distance." She shook her head. "I didn't have a chance to learn the whys, the hows, and the emotions behind any of them. *You* didn't give me that opportunity." A beat. "The difference is that I was willing to give you the time and space to figure them out along with the *patience* and understanding for you to share them on your terms."

"Trix—"

"So, fuck you, Jet. Fuck you for calling me damaged. Fuck you for me not being able to live up to your impossible standards." She sucked in a breath and straightened. "And fuck you, for not loving me the way you should have."

With that, she slammed the door and walked away.

Fuck him.

Fuck Jet.

Fuck. It. All.

TEN

Jet

HE SLAMMED his hand on the steering wheel. "Fucking hell."

What the hell was wrong with that woman? Accusing him of being a coward. Was she actually serious? Jet threw open the door and got out, striding angrily over to the elevator and swiping his key fob.

"Impossible woman," he muttered. "Trying to make this seem like my fault—"

The elevator doors opened, and he froze, eyes unseeing as her earlier words washed over him.

You didn't fight for us.

The reason you didn't do any of those things was because you were scared.

Fuck you for not loving me the way you should have.

All of his words, including his so-called apology, crystalized into a perfect representation . . . of his asshole-ness.

Fuck. Trix was right. One hundred percent right.

He'd been *all* of the things she'd mentioned. Scared, cowardly, impatient. But the one that stung the most was the fact that he *hadn't* loved her enough, hadn't loved her the way he should have.

If he had . . .

Fuck it all, if he *had* he wouldn't have said those things today, wouldn't have left her the way he had, wouldn't have acted like such a—

"Shit," he muttered, spinning back in the direction of the parking lot.

He needed to go after her, to apologize and actually mean it this time.

But fuck, where had she gone? He'd all but kidnapped her, intending to take her back to his place and force some food in her over a movie, to try and distract her from what had happened, and now he'd run her off by being a total—

Twatwaffle.

"Shit," he muttered again, hurrying up the driveway and out onto the street. Trix was nowhere in sight, so he strode down the block, searching for an exhausted brunette in scrubs.

Nothing. Nothing. Noth—

There.

Thank fuck.

He rushed over. "Trix," he said. "I—"

She spun one-hundred-eighty degrees, not saying a word, not acknowledging him in any way. Instead, she lifted her phone to her face, and he saw that she'd ordered a Lyft.

More guilt. This time adding in the fact that she was paying for a ride home.

But at least he could solve this one.

He reached over her shoulder and snagged her cell, walking quickly back toward his building.

"What the fuck, Jet?" Trix exclaimed, chasing after him. Not answering, he rounded the corner and headed for the lobby of his building. "Give me my phone back," she snapped. "Now."

Jet opened the door, held it wide for her to precede him.

She stopped, glaring and reaching for her cell.

His only answer was to stow it safely in his pocket.

Trix studied him, seemed to be debating between making a scene by attempting to wrestle the phone from him or walking through the door he held open.

After a few seconds, she strode through the door.

"Jet," she growled when he walked past her and hit the button for the elevator.

He still didn't reply, mostly because he didn't know what to say. His thoughts were swirling with her words, with what he'd realized, and the realization that he couldn't begin to make up for everything he said to her.

He'd called her damaged, for fuck's sake.

That was the pot calling the kettle black.

He still revolted against using the money his parents had left him, had done his damnedest to do the exact opposite of what they wanted for him for years. Hell, even putting typical teenaged revolt aside, he hadn't discussed his parents with Trix at all, aside from the barest details about their deaths.

And yet he'd spent the last three years pretending he was both the victim and the person in the right.

Fuck, everyone always said that hindsight was twenty-twenty, but it still stung like hell to realize how truly screwed up he was.

Damaged.

Fuck.

The doors opened, and Trix glanced up at him when he held them open. He didn't move, didn't do anything except hold them. With another long-suffering sigh, she got on.

He pushed the button for his floor, half-expecting her to dart off.

But instead, she leaned back against the wall and crossed

her arms. Her eyes were as dark as rain clouds as she glared at him, fury pulling her brows down. One pissed-off—and well-deserved—woman threatening to dismember him with her stare, and she'd never been more beautiful.

Just like every other time he was in her presence, whether it had been that restaurant a few weeks ago, the hospital that day, Syria a few years before, every nerve in his body instinctively knew where she was.

It was like the heightened awareness of sensing when danger was near.

Except, it wasn't danger he was feeling.

Or at least, not the life-threatening type, proverbial dismembering glare aside.

Blinders. He'd gone a long time wearing them, not understanding the consequences, or perhaps, not being open to the fact that he'd played a role in them right alongside Trix. And that made him weak and cowardly and frankly, he was disgusted with himself.

But how to explain that?

How to prove to her that despite the bullshit he'd said not an hour before, he understood now that he'd been so incredibly wrong?

Yet, if someone came to him with that, flipping their opinions on a head after less than an hour, he'd tell them to fuck off and never come back. So, how to get her to understand that while he was still digesting the realization, he understood he was wrong, that he'd seriously fucked up, and though he'd stopped short of accepting responsibility for his part in the demise of their relationship before, he was ready to take ownership now.

All the right words.

All the right sentiments.

He wouldn't believe a fucking word of them.

Fuck.

But before he could go around in another circle in his mind, the elevator dinged, and the doors opened. Trix strode off, chin high, shoulders straight, backpack secured over both shoulders.

He should have taken that, too, so she didn't have to haul it so far.

Another should have, could have.

Ugh.

She stopped just inside the hall and looked—okay, *glared*—at him. But Jet was already committed to this fruitless (probably) venture, and so he slipped past Trix and headed down the hall to his condo's door.

Less than a minute later, he'd unlocked it and they were both inside, her backpack propped just beyond the threshold.

"Can I get you a glass of wine?"

One brown brow lifted.

Despite everything—the guilt, the disappointment, the frustration—that arched eyebrow had him biting back a smile, and he relaxed. Slightly. He'd lay it out there and not expect her to forgive him because . . . how could he?

"I'm trying to butter you up before I eat crow."

She turned on her heel and walked toward the windows. "You need to eat a fuck-ton more than crow. I'm talking fucking bald eagle level crow."

It was snark and her tone was acerbic, but it was what was underneath that surface level toughness that really sliced him to the quick. He'd hurt her, wounded her deeply.

"I'm sorry."

The second time that evening he'd said those words, but the first time he actually understood all he was apologizing for.

Trix turned, eyes searching his face for a long moment. Then she shrugged and rotated back to face the windows again. "Apology accepted." A beat. "Can I have my cell back now?"

Jet stifled a sigh and moved to the kitchen, pulling down two wine glasses—thanks Target—from a cabinet and a bottle of Zinfandel from the fridge. He remembered she'd mentioned liking it years before, and now he had to wonder how much of his blithely walking the aisles of the giant home goods store had been because he'd been trying to set up a house for himself and how much had been him knowing that with the two of them being in the same city, the same workplace, they would always have ended up in this exact place.

Though, if he was admitting every single one of his deepest, darkest secrets, he would have said that when he'd imagined Trix in his condo, he hadn't expected her to be quite so pissed at him.

He found the bottle opener, poured them each a glass, and then took a seat on one side of his island on one of his newly arrived barstools, his wine in front of him, Trix's glass on the opposite side.

Silence.

Still staring out the windows, Trix sighed. "Are you going to tell me why you've all but kidnapped me?"

"You followed me here," he pointed out, partly because it was true, but mostly because he hoped that it would piss her off and prompt her to face him.

The second worked.

Maybe too well.

"You know what?" she asked, throwing up her hands. "Keep my phone. I'll get a taxi." She moved to the door.

He jumped out of his chair and caught her arm. "Trix."

She wrenched out of his grip. "Fuck you, Jet."

"I deserve that," he said. "And more—"

"And another thing," she snapped, jabbing him in the chest with her finger, "you deserve a hell of a lot more than a *fuck you* after the shit you said tonight—"

"You're right."

"You were a fucking jerk, s-saying those things." At that slight falter, she tilted her head up toward the ceiling, eyes sliding closed. One breath in and out. Another. Then one more. Her face dropped back down, stare meeting his. "They were out of line, and I can never forgive you for them."

That made his stomach churn, but it wasn't anything less than he deserved. "I understand."

"So, then give me my phone and let me go."

He bent slightly, bringing his face very close to hers. "I can't."

Her tongue darted out, wetting her lips and drawing his focus there, to how much he was desperate to kiss her. Her pupils widened, shaky exhale escaping. He leaned in and—

No.

He couldn't.

He reached into his pocket and pulled out her cell. "I was beyond unfair and a total asshole. It was easier to blame you than admit I was scared to be in a relationship where I might care for someone more than they cared for me."

Jet clenched his hands into fists at his sides. "You were right. My parents were shit, and I never felt loved or like I was good enough to meet their exacting standards. But I didn't tell you that because . . . well, I don't know if it was because I didn't want to look weak or because I hadn't come to terms with it or if I was living in denial."

He gave in to the urge to touch Trix and gently cupped her cheek. "Neither of us was very good at sharing what was beneath our armor, but it was both of us, and for me to blame you wasn't right."

His chest was heaving, she was staring up at him with wide eyes, and their mouths were barely a few inches apart.

Jet bit back the urge to kiss her.

Instead, he picked up her palm and put her cell in her hand then bent, picked up her backpack, and gently set it on her shoulders.

"I know this isn't nearly enough to excuse how I left, what I said tonight, but I hope you'll believe me when I say I finally have clarity and that I really am sorry."

With that, he turned away, heading back into the kitchen. He grabbed his glass, mostly so he'd have something to do with his hands that didn't involve going back over to Trix, hauling her close, and slanting his mouth across hers.

First, that would get him slapped.

Second . . . that would get him slapped.

Smothering a sigh, he crossed to the windows and stared out at the city. The sun had gone down, only smudges of red and orange remaining as the navy and black of the evening crept forward over the sky. The buildings were mostly shadows, some lights on inside the nearby residential and office spaces, but many were darkened at this hour. Crimson taillights crawled through the skitter-scattered streets below, some sort of perverse version of Pac-Man.

And it was still odd.

To be in this busy of a city after so much time away.

He heard the thud of the door closing and let his shoulders drop, the glass of un-tasted wine descending to hang by his side.

Jet didn't know what he'd been hoping for.

Some miracle where he said he was sorry and Trix automatically forgave him and then launched herself into his arms and they made love beneath the moonlight?

He snorted.

Sure. Of course, it would happen that way.

Except, this was the real world and he'd fucked up, and things didn't always magically work out just because someone apologized. Plus, he didn't even know what he wanted and—

Lie.

A sigh.

Yes, that was a lie, and even though his conscience was a giant pain in the ass, it was still an untruth. For all their issues, Trix was the one woman he'd never been able to get out of his head.

He'd always thought about her—whether it was on a particularly tough case where it would have been wonderful to have her at his side, or what she'd smelled like after a shower—that tropical floral scent—or how she'd woken—slowly, incrementally, like a cat stretching after having been woken up from a nap.

He remembered how she'd kissed, how she held him tightly when he'd thrust home.

He remembered her joy at saving a baby in sub-Saharan Africa, her sadness in losing the baby's mother.

He remembered—

Everything.

Now they were together again, and he'd blown it . . . again.

"Fuck," he muttered.

"You know, generally, it's better to drink a Zinfandel cold rather than letting it sit out at room temperature."

He whipped around so fast that the wine in question splashed out of the glass, dripping down off his fingers and onto the carpet.

She hadn't gone.

The thud had been her backpack hitting the floor near the barstool, her sneakers silent as they'd traveled across the carpet.

He opened his mouth.

She shook her head. "I'm sorry, too."

"But, Trix—"

"Not tonight," she said. "I'll rake you over the coals again some other time." She lifted the glass to her lips and took a sip, eyes sliding closed, an approving hum escaping her mouth.

His cock twitched.

Not a surprise since it *was* Trix.

But then her pale lids peeled back, and her gray eyes met his. "Can we just be us again? For tonight, can we just pretend none of the bad stuff happened?"

Now his cock wasn't the affected organ. Instead, his heart rolled over in his chest, the vulnerable underbelly exposed and throbbing. How had he ever thought this woman wasn't worth the effort of peeling back the layers?

His eyes dropped to his feet, regret tearing through him again.

"Please, Jet?"

And because she asked, he tucked the emotions down, forced his gaze to meet hers again. "Yeah, sweetheart. We can just be us again."

An *us*.

He'd been an idiot in a multitude of ways, but perhaps the stupidest thing he'd done was not realizing quite how much he wanted them to be an *us* again.

Well, he burned that bridge quite thoroughly, and there was no going back.

But, part of him couldn't help but hope, maybe if they couldn't go back, they could still move forward.

ELEVEN

Trix

SHE SAT across the island from Jet and felt like a total idiot.

She could have left. She *should* have left.

But there had just been something so sad and arresting about the way he'd stood staring out the windows. All alone. She'd watched him stand there, and her fury had faded away. In its place was . . . not compassion, exactly, but understanding or maybe clarity.

They'd hurt each other.

They'd both said things that weren't kind.

They'd both made mistakes.

They were both very much alone.

Trix knew that feeling, looking out upon the world and not knowing one's place, standing on the outside and wondering how to make it different, how to slip inside. God, she knew it too fucking well, knew how it made her heart ache with longing, her mind cloud with sadness. A person wasn't designed to be alone forever. At some point that separation grew painful and they needed—

Connection.

Love.

Affection.

Friendship.

Plus, he'd opened a bottle of Zinfandel. She couldn't let that go to waste, especially when he'd even had it chilling in the fridge, allowing the sweet notes to sing but not overwhelm the palate.

Yes, she'd spent ten years abroad.

Yes, she still knew her wine.

Mostly because—

"Do you know why I like Zinfandel?" she asked when he sat across from her, setting the glass on the granite surface.

"No," he murmured, still appearing a little shell-shocked that she was still there. Hell, she was a little surprised herself, but she was also sad about Tom and though she also felt rubbed raw from Jet's words, he'd also apologized.

She wasn't one to hold a grudge for too long.

Take ownership, say sorry, don't do the behavior again, and everyone moves on.

Probably why she'd been hurt so often by her family.

Heather excluded, they could apologize till they were blue in the face, sometimes even pretend to change and take responsibility, but in the end, it always circled right back around—she was disappointed, they were themselves.

That was the way of life.

And maybe it made her a pushover, but she never could stop herself from giving a person another chance.

Probably also why her walls were so thick.

Don't allow anyone too close because they will inevitably fail you.

Such happy thoughts.

A warm palm settled over her hand. "Did you want to tell me why you liked Zinfandel so much?"

Not really now, but she'd brought the subject up, so she'd go with it.

"My father bought the winery when I was in high school." He nodded when she glanced up. "Even though I wasn't drinking age yet, I thought I could make myself useful by learning about the grape varieties being grown there, what types of wine were being made." She smiled ruefully. "I could name every variety and their preferred soil type, fertilizer, and growing season before I could legally take a drink. But when I was actually legal and could go on tastings, it turned out I could actually only stomach a couple of types."

"Zinfandel being one of them?"

She smiled ruefully. "I apparently have a sweet tooth, even in wine."

"I remember," he said. "I think you tried every type of chocolate bar from every place we visited."

"The airport shops didn't offer much else in most of them."

"True."

He brought his hand back and used it to raise his glass to his lips. "I seem to remember that you like champagne."

A laugh. "Only the expensive kind, remember?" She smiled. "How much was that bottle again?"

"Three hundred and fifty bucks." Jet grinned. "I almost fainted when we got the bill. Here I am, a simple man making a limited salary. We find ourselves in New York for a night, and I want to take my girlfriend out for a nice night."

She shrugged, lips twitching. "I made it worth it."

"You did," he agreed, smiling back at her. "I just nearly had to sell a kidney to be able to afford it."

Trix glanced around the condo, not having had to grow up with a billionaire father to know the place was expensive. San

Francisco real estate prices were outrageous, add in the door-
man, the parking, the expensive kitchen, and the spacious living
area, and this was in the multimillion-dollar range.

Plus, the HOA fees had to be off the charts.

"You seem to be doing okay," she said. "This kitchen alone is
bigger than my apartment on the whole."

A shadow crossed his expression, and Trix prepared to be
cut down, or at least told to mind her own business. Instead, the
darkness left his face and he flattened his palms on the granite.

"My parents were like yours in a way. Lots of money, still
critically unhappy."

Her heart skipped a beat.

"You know they passed," he said, and she nodded, remem-
bering him telling her they'd both been killed in a car accident.
"I bought the condo with the money they left me." He sighed.
"After promising myself I'd never actually touch it."

She frowned. "But why? They wanted you to have—"

"They used it to control me." His fingers tapped on the
granite. "Everything was a game, a test, a challenge. Even my
allowance or paying for tuition. I always had to prove myself
worthy to get it." He glanced up and his dark brown eyes met
hers. "Did you know I never heard my father say *I love you?* Not
once in my entire life."

It was her turn to cover his hand. "I'm sorry, Jet. I didn't—"

"Know?" he finished when she stopped herself. Trix
nodded. "Well, no one knew. I didn't want to be that kid, the
pathetic one looking for love, begging for it. I"—he shook his
head—"I couldn't allow myself to be that person. For many
reasons."

She wanted to ask about the reasons, but didn't have the
courage that night.

She didn't want to be shot down, not when he'd shared
something so big, not when *she'd* shared something big, too.

So instead, Trix said, "Parents suck."

He grinned, turned his hand over so their fingers interlaced. "I'm guessing your dad was about as impressed by your wine knowledge as mine was about my MCAT score?"

"Depends," she said. "What was your score?"

A squeeze of their fingers. "I'm guessing yours was higher."

She took a sip of wine, knew that hers was good. "526."

His eyes widened. "You missed two fucking points? That's it? Two off the whole thing?"

Trix shrugged, cheeks feeling a little warm.

"I took it three times to get a 512."

"I feel like this is the doctor's equivalent of whose penis is bigger." They both laughed and she took another sip of her wine, her head starting to feel pleasantly fuzzy. "Who cares? Scores aside, you went to medical school, I didn't."

Sad chocolate eyes on hers. "You should have gone."

Trix shrugged. "I couldn't have afforded it for a variety of reasons," she said. "Plus, I'm happy being a nurse." Her lips quirked. "Hell, with all the overtime I've been pulling, I think my salary is bigger than yours."

Jet laughed. "Probably." A beat. "Want to order something for dinner?"

Her heart twisted, and she carefully set her glass down on the counter. "I should probably go."

He nodded. "Yeah," he said. "Let me grab my keys, I'll drive you back to the hospital."

She shook her head, standing and heading for the door. "No, it's only a few minutes by Lyft. I'll be fine."

"I'm not making you pay for a ride when I all but kidnapped you."

"The kidnapping part is true," she agreed. "But I think it's good that we got the stuff out, don't you? Now we can move on." She meant it, too. What he'd said had hurt. Majorly. But maybe also, now that she'd told him a lot of what she'd felt and he'd *definitely* gotten out what was on his chest, they could go forward as friends.

She missed her friend Jet.

"I don't know if there could possibly be anything good about what I said." He'd stood, his hands fisted at his side.

Trix moved back around the island, standing next to his barstool and reaching for one of his fists. "No, there's not."

His eyes bored into hers, regret in their depths. She didn't understand what had changed so abruptly, but she'd learned after working in the medical field for the last decade that life was short and fragile and fleeting, that sometimes a person had to let go, to surrender to their instincts, and just live.

Nothing was served by letting the hurt from the past eat her alive.

So, she was going to let go, move on, and—

"I'm—"

"No more sorrys," she said. "Just don't be a dick, and we'll be fine."

"I'll make it up to you."

Jet's expression was earnest now, and he flipped his hand over so that their fingers were linked once again. God, even that simple touch felt good. Trix hadn't realized how much she'd missed touching another person, not to administer care or hurt them by cleaning a wound or starting an IV, but just for comfort or because it felt good or—

"I should go."

"I'll drive you."

She pulled back. "No, Jet."

Chocolate eyes on hers for a long time, and she prepared herself to stand firm against his argument. She was exhausted after the shift, after the argument, and the wine hadn't helped. Bed was calling, even more heavily than food.

He dropped his hand, nodded. "Will you text me when you get home?"

"I don't have your number."

His lips curved up. "We can remedy that." He held out a hand. "I can plug my number in."

Hesitancy slid through her, and she clutched her cell against her chest. "Are you going to try and keep my cell again?"

More curving, revealing a slice of white teeth. "Not this time," he said and leaned close enough to bump his shoulder against hers. "Come on, I won't even hold it. I'll just watch as you plug in the numbers to make sure you put it in right."

She narrowed her eyes.

His affected innocence.

A sigh. "Fine."

Victory slid across his face, but his tone was neutral as he recited his number.

"Can I walk you to the lobby?"

"Nope."

"Wait until the Lyft comes?"

Trix shook her head. "Nope."

"Can I at least pay for—" He reached for his wallet.

"Absolutely, not," she said and snatched up her backpack as she headed for the door. "Watch out the window if you're worried."

"This is the wrong side. The lobby—"

"We can't all have everything."

Jet rolled his eyes. "And even if it was, what am I going to do from twenty floors up?"

"Play Superman?"

His only response was to shake his head.

She reached for the door handle. "Bye, Jet."

"Bye, Trix."

He held the door open for her, and she strode out and down

the hall to the elevator. But he didn't go back inside until she got onto the car. At her hard look, he just grinned and waved. "Didn't promise not to watch you make it down the hall."

Trix sighed, hit the button for the lobby, and shook her head.

"Night," she called.

"Goodnight, sweetheart," he said just as the elevator doors shut.

That *sweetheart* stayed with her all the way through the ride back to the hospital, it followed her home and clung close as she powered through a bowl of cereal.

She heard it again just as her head hit the pillow.

And the husky endearment that soothed the raw edges of the hurt inside her was still nearby when she woke up the next morning.

TWELVE

Jet

HE BROUGHT Trix coffee to the hospital the next morning—an Americano with just a splash of cream. Meanwhile, his was diluted with four sugars and several healthy splashes of cream.

"It'll put hair on your chest," he teased, handing it over as she got out of the car.

This gave him two things—one, it distracted her from the fact that he'd been lying in wait near where she liked to park for the last fifteen minutes and two, with her hands busy bringing the coffee to her mouth, he snagged her backpack from the passenger's seat.

Her mouth opened on a sigh—caffeine-related, he thought, rather than the fact that he'd grabbed her heavy bag—and he took that as a victory.

"Just what I always needed," she said, lips quirking. "More hair on my chest."

He chuckled, shrugged on her backpack. "What do you have in here?"

"Is this where you fill in the blank with bricks?"

"I've got my dad jokes on point."

Smiling, she slammed her door, walked alongside him into the hospital. "Do you want to be one?"

He paused, eyes slanting down to her. "Want to be what?"

"A dad," she said, nudging him to the side and using her pass on the employee entrance.

"Thanks," he murmured. "And yes, I do want to be a father. I thought for a long time I didn't want to be, but . . . despite recent events, I think I'd be an okay one."

She touched his arm. "You've always been great with kids."

Not letting his behavior off the hook, but not sticking the knife in and twisting it. How had he been so blind to not realize how incredible she was?

Or maybe, like Trix had said, he'd known she was everything he wanted, but deep inside, he'd been too scared to truly accept that she was all of the things he'd wanted, and so he'd made up excuses to push her away, so he didn't put himself out there.

Too deep for this early in the morning.

And yet, he'd thought about little else except what he'd been thinking three years ago, the untruths he'd held on to since then.

"What about you?" he asked as they made their way down the hall.

"I didn't really think much about it for a long time," she murmured. "But I've always pictured myself married and with kids someday." Her eyes danced when she glanced up at him. "We're getting older now, though, so I guess someday is getting closer."

"True," he teased and tugged the end of her ponytail. "I think I even see a few gray hairs in here."

She smacked his hand away. "Rude."

He snorted and their entrance to the break room was significantly less eventful than the previous day. He slipped her bag from his shoulders and passed it over.

"Thanks," she said.

"No prob," he said.

They stowed their things then stared at each other for a moment—a long, awkward moment.

"Well," she eventually said, slipping off her sweatshirt and stashing it in her locker, "I'm going to go."

He didn't have anything smart or witty to say to that and so he settled on, "Yeah." Then watched her ponytail flutter behind her as her head bobbed and she spun away.

A second later she was out the door.

But he hadn't insulted her.

So Jet was counting that as a win.

It was Tuesday at lunchtime and when he pushed through the door into the break room, Trix was sitting at the table, reading a book, her lunch spread out in front of her.

She glanced up, those pretty gray eyes meeting his. "Hey."

He grabbed his lunch from the fridge, his cell from his locker, and hesitated. He and Trix had come to a tentative peace and he didn't want to overstep.

"I won't bite," she said. "Promise."

Jet grinned and sat down across from her, pulling out his very original PB&J and side salad he'd picked up from the cafeteria the day before but hadn't had a chance to eat.

So fine, his cooking skills weren't all that great.

But it was food and it would work.

He started in on the green stuff, silently scrolling through his phone, not wanting to interrupt Trix while she read, while also not really knowing what to say.

Trix closed the book and he saw that it wasn't so much a book as a guide.

For Alcatraz.

His brows shot up. "Have you never gone?"

She shook her head. "We didn't really do touristy stuff growing up."

There was a lot to unpack in that statement. A lot of undertones that went along with it, plenty of subtly Jet was just starting to understand had always been there in the first place.

"It's expensive," he said, knowing she'd mentioned that funds hadn't exactly been flush growing up.

"Yeah." She picked up her sandwich. "But it was more than that. My mom didn't want to do it"—a shrug—"which, in my house, meant it didn't happen."

He put down his fork. "That happened in my house, too," he murmured.

"Yeah." She nodded, took a bite, eyes glued to the pamphlet. "I'm going tomorrow actually. It's silly to go on my one day off this week, but I promised myself I'd start doing some of the stuff I missed out on and—"

"I've never been either," he blurted.

She paused, eyes flicking between the pamphlet and him. "Did you . . . um . . . did you want to come with—"

"Yes," he said instantly.

Her lips curved, expression warming. "Okay. I'm leaving about nine. Want me to pick you up from your place?"

"Works for me."

Teeth nibbling on her bottom lip, sandwich still clutched in her fingers. Knowing her break was almost over, Jet forced himself to shift focus. He didn't want her to miss her chance to eat, and so he began talking about the case he'd seen that morning. Discussing numbers and symptoms, asking her opinion, getting her perspective. It wasn't a technique to change the conversation away from personal so much as he wanted her to relax enough to go back to her meal and that her insights were always valuable.

And it worked.

Her shoulders lowered, her expression lost its hint of weariness.

They talked for much of the next fifteen minutes before she had to go back on. They discussed work and joked about funny things that had happened so far during the shift.

And Trix ate.

Small victories, but they were rebuilding their connections and so Jet would take it.

Fifteen minutes at a time.

His phone buzzed with a text saying Trix was out front and Jet hurried through the front doors of the lobby, pushing out onto the sidewalk and taking a few moments to spot her car.

He tugged open the passenger's side, sat down, and extended the cup of coffee.

Trix's eyes were excited, though tired, but when she saw the coffee, they brightened. "You're a god."

"I also have donuts," he said, holding up the white bag.

"I stand by my statement," she said, snagging one before checking traffic and pulling out onto the road.

It took a while to reach the Embarcadero, morning traffic slowing them down, but Jet didn't mind. Not when it gave him and Trix some time to ease past the awkwardness. They weren't quite back to their old pattern of banter and teasing, but they'd made progress.

They shot the shit about traffic and how it had been different in the places they'd traveled to until they parked and then about the places they *hadn't* gotten to and still wanted to visit on the ferry ride across, then caught up on what they knew was happening in some of their old colleagues' lives in line to get the audio tour. That was when they quieted down, listening to the story of the supposedly inescapable prison and the mystery of the three men who managed to get off The Rock.

"What do you think?" Trix asked, walking next to him as they headed down the gangway leading to the ferry that would take them to the city. "Did they survive?"

Jet shrugged. "It seems unlikely they survived the cold water and strong currents. What about you? Did they pull a Nick Cage and get off The Rock?"

She made a face as they went out onto the open deck, the ferry pulling away from the small island. "I'm not sure. I mean, kids make the swim all the time. It's not far. But in the dark, not knowing where they were going? I don't think they could have."

As she'd talked, she'd rotated around, watching them sail across the bay. Wind whipped up around them, tugging at the ends of the brown ponytail.

Jet's fingers itched to touch, to see if they felt as soft as he remembered.

But she hadn't given him permission to touch.

So he contented himself with leaning up against the rail next to her and continuing to try and puzzle out the rest of the mystery.

Just like he wanted to puzzle out the mystery of Trix.

Time. Patience. Care.

She deserved that much from him.

So he didn't touch, but he *did* tease and talk about the bad reality shows she was watching—promising to watch one about people who decided to get married without seeing each other— and then when they docked, he tempted her into the quintessential lunch of clam chowder in a sourdough bread bowl.

Jet argued with her about buying her a San Francisco emblazoned sweatshirt and then bought it anyway.

Though, he did relent and let her buy him some saltwater taffy.

He hated saltwater taffy.

But he didn't hate spending time with Trix.

***

THE NEXT WEEK PASSED UNEVENTFULLY. He continued to bring Trix coffee every morning when they were on shift together, kept their interactions light and easy, and while there weren't any more touristy days, there also weren't any fireworks between them.

Plus, their day to Alcatraz had eliminated a lot of the awkwardness. So, bonus.

They chatted while at work to pass the slow time between admissions, tag-teamed difficult patients, and generally recreated the connection they'd built when they'd first met abroad.

And it was just as good now as it was then.

If he'd needed confirmation that he'd been an idiot, then this week would have proved it to him. But he'd already known that, and so it did nothing more than confirm he was doing the right thing.

His phone rang as he headed out to his car, having stayed later than Trix that evening. He'd been waiting on some test results to come back, wanting to make sure he'd made the right call before admitting the patient he'd been working on—and considering the CT had shown the man had a brain bleed, Jet was glad he'd stayed.

"Hello?" he said, bringing his cell up to his ear.

"I hope you were serious about wanting that family," Clay

said. "Because Heather apparently has found the perfect woman for you."

Was that woman Trix?

If not, he could guarantee she wasn't.

"She—" There was a grunt and then muffled voices. "Hey —" Clay's voice cut off a second time, a scuffle loud enough to make him wince came over the airwaves, and then a cheerful female voice came on.

"Jet? It's Heather."

He grinned as he unlocked his car and sat down in the driver's seat. "Hey, Heather."

Keys in the ignition, doors locked, call on Bluetooth.

"Listen," Heather said. "I have the perfect woman for you. Her name is Molly, and she owns a local restaurant. The food is off the charts. She's sweet, she's funny, she's—"

"Heather."

Her words cut off.

"I appreciate the thought but—"

"I know that you and Trix didn't hit it off like we'd hoped. She mentioned that things were fine, but there wasn't a spark."

That made Jet's teeth clench together. "I didn't—"

"It doesn't matter. I get it. No doctor-nurse fantasy come to life, but—"

"That's not—"

Heather's affronted sigh was loud. "Look, you told Clay you wanted to find someone to build a future with. If that's not something you want—"

"I wasn't lying," he said. "I *am* looking to settle down."

"And what? You're too good for someone who works in a restaurant?"

He backed out of the spot and exited the parking lot, navigating his way out into traffic. "I'm not too good for anyone," he said. "I just . . ."

"What?" she snapped.

"I've already met someone."

Her tone immediately warmed. "Oh, that's great news. Who is it?"

Jet waffled for a minute then decided that since he'd already pulled his head out of his ass as far as Trix was concerned, he might be able to use her sister to help him secure another chance.

Because that was what this last week had shown him, that bottom line, his life was better with Trix in it.

Easy. Decision made.

Now how to convince Trix to give him another shot?

Jet was thinking that maybe Heather could help.

"It's Trix," he said when she made an impatient sound, and then he had the rarefied distinction of silencing Heather O'Keith. For a few moments, at least. Because she was smart and quick and never was knocked down for long—whether it was shock or in the business world.

"But Trix said—"

"We dated when we were working for Doctors without Borders."

More silence. Then, "Um, what?"

"We were together a year. I seriously fucked up. I—well, that's between her and me, but I wasn't thinking clearly. I said some shit, purposefully got reassigned away from her, and now . . ."

Sharp edges to her words. "Now, what?"

He deserved the tone and also knew that as Trix's sister, Heather would need reassurance that his heart was in the right place, that he'd recognized his mistakes and wanted to make them right.

"I'm not saying that we both didn't contribute to our breakup," he said. "But I certainly deserve the lion's share of the blame. I fucked up, Heather. It was easier for me to pretend that Trix was at fault, but I know now that's not the case."

"Hmm."

"I've apologized," he said. "And I'll continue to do my best to make it up to her, but . . ."

"You blew it."

"I overreacted. I cost us three years. I want—" He shook his head and pulled into the garage. "I guess I just want to prove that I deserve another shot with her."

"I think that's up to Trix to decide." Still frosty, but not quite as sharp.

A dulled arrow.

Still deadly, but marginally less effective.

"I agree," he murmured. "But she says we're friends now, that we'll forget the past and move forward."

"Sounds like she made her decision," Heather pointed out. "And that you're lucky to have her friendship at all."

Jet was starting to feel desperate now. Mostly because Heather was right. Trix had been gracious enough to apologize to him, and she'd never denied her past's role in their relationship—he got to shoulder the asshole burden on that front. First, for holding it against her and second, for doing such a piss-poor job of telling her he was sorry.

"I *am* lucky she gave me that much."

"Right," Heather said. "I'll give the phone back to Clay now. Let me know at some point if you want to go out with Molly—"

"I love her!" he blurted loud enough to make himself jump.

And he didn't think he would have been able to quantify what he was feeling into those words if he hadn't been so damned worried about Heather hanging up on him.

Probably her intention.

"Hmm," she murmured.

"Heather—"

"I know something about overreacting, unthinking men," she began.

"Hey!" he heard Clay say in the background. "I didn't—"

"*Anyway*," Heather went on, "my point is that people make mistakes. I get that. But I'm not willing to go behind my sister's back and betray her trust." She sucked in a breath. "I just got her back, Jet. I don't want to do something to make her leave again."

"Me neither," he said.

"So, I think I have to leave this up to—"

"I'm just asking for one thing," he said quickly, "and then if it doesn't work, I'll leave it alone. I'll even go on a date with Molly. O-or whoever else you want. I just need one shot. Pl—"

"What's the one thing?"

He told her.

Then waited for an interminable moment when all he heard was, "Hmm."

But just when he'd given up hope, Heather chuckled and said, "I'm probably going to Hell for this, but okay."

Jet breathed out a sigh of relief. "I promise that I'll never hurt your sister again."

There was a pause and then Heather said, "No one can make that promise, Jet. I just need you to love her like she deserves." His heart twisted. "If you can do that, I'll do the favor you asked for."

"I will."

No hesitation or reservations. No more waffling.

He'd made a decision, and Trix deserved the best he could offer.

"Okay, then," Heather said. "How do you want to begin?"

THIRTEEN

Trix

"GO ON ANOTHER BLIND DATE, they said," Trix grumbled, straightening the straps on her little black dress before slipping on her heels. "Because the first one went so well."

Yup. She was an idiot, but Heather had called and begged and cajoled and . . . Trix was going on another blind date.

Awesome.

Couldn't wait.

Rolling her eyes and wondering why she'd let her sister talk her into this, Trix picked up her purse and headed to the door.

She should be looking forward to the date with the gorgeous engineer, Monroe, that Heather knew via her work connections, but Trix just couldn't summon up the energy to be excited, even after seeing the man's picture.

Tall, dark, and gorgeous.

Exactly her type.

Except—

He wasn't Jet.

And *that* was a problem. Because, yes, she'd forgiven Jet for what he'd said, and they'd both taken ownership for the way their relationship had imploded. They'd moved on as friends . . . exactly as she'd wanted.

So there should be nothing wrong with her going on a date, and she certainly shouldn't be wanting that date to be Jet.

Friends.

That was it.

That was safer.

Her inner bullshit detector blared with that last thought, because she wasn't supposed to be making herself safer. She was supposed to be putting herself out there, being vulnerable, actually living her life.

Not safely.

"Ugh," she muttered and pushed out her front door. It wasn't even like Jet seemed to be interested in anything more than friendship at this point.

It had been just over two weeks since the almost kiss in the break room, nearly two months since the actual one, and he hadn't given her one heated look or lover-like caress or let his mouth come very near hers.

Absolutely nothing to indicate that he wanted her in a more-than-a-friend way.

She needed to move on.

Accept that his urge to fuck her had been closely tied with his anger about their relationship and now that the past and its ties were resolved, his desire had disappeared along with any ill feelings.

So, Date Night.

As in, she'd *finally* accepted Heather's set up and was going to get on with it, just mildly less "blind"—since she had seen the man in question's photo.

That would have solved a lot of problems for her before the last one.

Snorting, she shook her head and walked to her car, her cell chirping in her purse just as she'd unlocked the doors.

"Hello?" she answered, not looking at the screen as she climbed in and turned on the ignition.

"Hey."

Her stomach fluttered at the sound of Jet's voice.

Friends, remember? Nothing more.

That was what she wanted, what Jet wanted based on how he'd been acting over the last couple of weeks.

Friends were great.

She was great.

Everything was great.

Trix snorted as she checked traffic and pulled out onto the road. "Hi," she said belatedly. "What's up?"

She and Jet had texted a little bit and talked on the phone a couple of times, so hearing his voice on the other end of the line didn't make her feel awkward and clam up. Still, her pulsed picked up, her thighs trembled, and her fingers tightened on the steering wheel.

"Not much," he said. "Do you want to grab a bite? Neither of us has to get up at the crack of dawn tomorrow."

Their shifts mostly lined up, except when Jet was on call or she picked up overtime. For example, this week she'd worked Wednesday through Saturday and had today and Monday off, grabbing some OT on Tuesday. Jet had worked that morning, but wouldn't work again until Wednesday.

But now they were both free and she was going on this stupid date, and so she wouldn't be able to grab dinner.

She mentally smacked herself.

She should be excited about the date, not feeling pouty about it.

"I can't," she said, trying to stifle the pouty as she pulled onto the freeway and not succeeding.

"Oh," he said, and the disappointment in his tone was audible. "No worries. I'll—"

"I have a date," she blurted.

"Uh—"

"I'd rather be eating with you than this joker Heather is setting me up with," she muttered. "He's having us go to some fancy French place, and all I want is tacos."

He snorted. "Tacos always win."

"I know!" she exclaimed. "But apparently he's trying to impress me." Yes, it was a grumble. Yes, it was uncharitable. No, she didn't care. "At least that's what Heather keeps reminding me. Meanwhile, I think she just enjoys torturing me."

"Siblings, I think, are good at that."

"You're lucky you don't have any."

He stifled a laugh. "You wouldn't have said that if you'd met my parents. You'd have said I could have used a barrier."

"I—" Trix stopped, not knowing what to say, except, "I know the feeling."

Silence.

Then, "I know you do, babe," he murmured then his voice rose. "Okay, rain check on dinner. Call me if your date goes sideways, and I'll open a can of whoop ass on the son of a bitch."

"He seems perfectly respectable," she countered.

"They always do," he muttered. "They always do."

She laughed. "'Night, Jet."

"Night, sweetheart."

Trix hung up, feeling even less like going on this date, but she wasn't an asshole. She determinedly put Jet from her mind and forced herself to head for the restaurant.

She didn't stand people up.

THE SAME COULD NOT BE SAID of the engineer she was supposed to be meeting.

Monroe was an asshole who'd stood her up.

Trix sat at the table, looking hot as hell in her little black dress, thank her very much, and . . . she'd been stood up.

Cool.

Note to the universe, she was going to kill her sister.

Especially since she'd texted Heather and hadn't gotten a response. "Probably enjoying herself with her stupidly beautiful husband in her stupidly beautiful house in her stupidly beautiful life," Trix muttered, eating the last piece of bread in the basket the waiter had brought her.

With a pitying look.

Ugh.

She was in full-force that night, too, having had the time to go to town on her hair and makeup. Plus, her body was on point, mostly thanks to too many shifts and a lack of time to eat the stash of junk food in her apartment, but the fact was that she looked good.

And it was utterly wasted.

Fucking men.

Trix signaled the waiter and he came over, that pitying expression still fixed to his face.

She repeated, *fucking men*.

"I think I'm ready for my check," she said.

His expression didn't change as he nodded and left, returning a few minutes later with the bill. He left to process her card—because who carried cash anymore? And if they did, then they were way more together than her, *plus* way more prepared for this particular situation than she was.

Her cell buzzed.

Sighing, she pulled it from her purse, expecting it to be Heather and readying her diatribe. Or even better, maybe it was Monroe, appropriately apologetic for having made her wait.

It was neither.

It was a text from Jet.

How goes the date?

She debated how to answer that, but then the waiter returned, and she was signing a receipt for an exorbitantly priced glass of wine and two pieces of bread.

Well, at least she wasn't at risk of bursting out of her dress.

Her phone buzzed again as she put on her coat.

Either that means it's going perfectly or it's gone to shit.

Her heels *click-clacked* across the pavement as she strode to where her car was parked—three freaking blocks away and in front of a fucking Mexican restaurant, of all places. Fate was really trying to fuck with her that evening.

She'd bypassed tacos and . . . gotten stood up.

Monroe was—

Buzz. Buzz.

Okay, I'm probably intruding, but now I'm worried. Let me know all is good by responding. If not, I'll assume the bastard turned out to be a serial killer and hunt you down.

She hesitated and then smiled begrudgingly.

A miserable, embarrassing night that had ended up with her alone on a San Franciscan street corner, and she was smiling.

This man.

Okay, universe. So maybe not *all* men were horrible.

Snorting, she tapped the screen a few times and lifted her phone to ear, listening to it ring a couple of times.

Then Jet was on the other end of the line and all was right in the world.

"Am I speaking to Trix or the serial killer?"

She laughed. "Trix. Unfortunately. A serial killer might not get stood up."

Silence. Then, "Seriously?"

"I don't want to say, yes, but . . ."

"Fucking bastard."

"I'm okay, Jet."

"Where are you now?"

"Walking to my car."

He sighed. "No, I mean, where *exactly* are you?"

"I—" She broke off.

"You," he countered. Then waited, and Trix felt a pulse of irritation slide through her. Partly because he was pushing, but mostly because he'd always been really good at out-patiencing her.

"Ugh." She blew out a breath, stifled her sigh and told him her cross street. "But I'm heading to my car which is parked near your building. Right by Molly's and that really good hole-in-the-wall Mexican place."

"Is this the Molly's that everyone is so excited about?"

"Have not you eaten there?" she asked, incredulous.

"No."

"I know," she said, pausing at a street corner to check for traffic and then crossing against the light. Citizens of San Francisco didn't wait on corners in the cold if cars weren't about to mow them down. She glanced, she walked, and she did it with confidence.

"What?" Jet asked.

"I know you haven't eaten there because otherwise, you would know exactly why Molly's is the shit. They have the best pear and gorgonzola salad with candied walnuts." She held her coat closed against a gust of wind. "I'd say something about liking those nuts in my mouth—"

He snorted.

"—but exactly that reaction," she said with a giggle, rounding the final corner to where her car was parked. "Molly's is delicious, and if you haven't eaten there, then you need to remedy it immediately."

"I'll take it under advisement."

"You should—"

Trix skittered to a stop when she saw what was leaning against her car. Or rather, *who* was resting a hip against her passenger's door, ankles crossed, a brown paper bag dangling from one hand, his cell pressed to his ear with the other.

Jet.

He pocketed the phone when she stopped, pushing off the car and coming toward her.

"I—" She shook her head. "What are you doing here?"

"I live here. Well, *there*." Jet smiled, jerked his head back over his shoulder.

"I remember," she grumbled.

Still smiling. "But the point is"—he held up the bag—"want to go up to my place and have tacos?"

Her jaw dropped open. "Um, what?"

"Did you eat?"

Another shake of her head.

"Good. I have tacos, let's go drink wine and eat them."

"I—"

He closed the distance between them and took her hand. "Stop thinking so hard. I've got chocolate ice cream in my freezer, a bag full of greasy deliciousness. Let's forget about the shitty night and do something fun."

That sounded like the best offer she'd heard all night. She rested her head on his shoulder, inhaled some of his yummy, spicy scent, and said, "Okay."

FOURTEEN

Jet

SHE'D SAID OKAY.

His heart leaped with joy, but he didn't gloat, or smirk, or tease her for accepting. Instead, he tightened his grip on her hand and started tugging her up to his condo. Quickly, before she changed her mind.

Less than five minutes later, she was in his condo and seated on a barstool with her favorite glass of wine and picking through the bag of food.

"Oh my God," she groaned and pulled out a burrito that was the size of her head. "You're a fucking god."

Jet bit back a smile.

He'd need to confess his part in the evening soon, but he figured it would be best to feed and water—or feed and alcohol —her first.

She pulled out three tacos, a bag of chips, along with guacamole and queso. "You sure bought a lot of food for yourself."

Yeah, he had.

Because the plan had always been to buy food for two.

"I can't believe that Monroe stood me up," she grumbled. "I waited in the restaurant for an hour, feeling pathetic with the waiters staring at me like I was a pity case." She pointed at the food. "Which do you want?"

Jet's gaze darted toward to the door, checking to make sure the dead bolt was thrown.

At least then he'd have a few extra seconds to stop her from storming out after he confessed his and Heather's part in this.

"Jet?"

"Hmm?"

"I'm starving. Did you want the burrito or the tacos?"

He moved to the fridge, pulled out a beer. "I don't care."

"Great." She grabbed the disposable wooden knife from the bag, sliced the burrito in half and took one taco then shoved the rest of the food in his direction. "We'll go, halvsies," she said, smiling up at him.

"Works for me."

Trix took a giant bite of burrito. "Mmm. God, I knew this place was good. I should have just skipped the date altogether and had this."

"This" sounded like "shmis" because she took another huge bite of burrito.

He smiled despite the guilt churning inside him.

He needed to own up—

She stopped, unbuttoned her coat, peeled it off, and tossed it over the back of the chair.

Which made his brain stop working.

She was wearing the dress from their blind date. *The* dress. The one that was low cut and skin tight and exposed the swirling, colorful lines tattooed on both arms. The dress left very little to the imagination. Imagination he didn't need because he had memories.

Memories that made his cock twitch.

Especially when she leaned forward to dig back into the burrito, and her breasts . . . *fuck*, but her breasts.

"Jet?"

"Hmm?"

Creamy skin, hard nipples in his mouth—

"Jet?"

He blinked. "Yeah?"

"You gonna eat?"

A nod and he moved jerkily to the stool. "Yeah." He picked up his half of the burrito and took a bite. "I like your dress."

Gray eyes on his, fire on their edges. "I seem to remember you making some comment about my *tits on display* the last time you saw me in this dress."

"I'm an asshole."

Silence.

His lips twitched. "Not going to disagree?"

"Nope." She lifted her arm to push back some of her hair and exposing the new tattoo he'd noticed a few weeks ago. But he'd only been able to see part of the curved blue and purple line then.

Now he saw the rest.

And his heart twisted. It was a stylized version of Odonnyew fie Kwan. The symbol basically meant that love never loses its way home and was a symbol of the Ashanti people of Ghana. "You got that?"

Her eyes shuttered. "Amare's brother did it for me." A shrug then a deliberate lightness in her tone. "Definitely not the most sanitary tattoo I've ever gotten, but still very meaningful."

He froze, dread circling in his gut at the underlying pain in her words. "When did you get it?"

Another shrug. "Doesn't matter."

"Trix."

She sighed. "That's why I was late coming home that night."

Shards of ice through his abdomen. There was no question as to what night she was referring to, at least not in his mind. She'd gotten it the night he'd left and—

"Do you like it?" she asked softly. "Don't think it's too much like cultural appropriation? I mean I wouldn't have gotten it at all, but Kwame said it was okay and Amare was so special and—"

He reached across the island and covered her hand. "I love your tattoos. Always have."

She stayed there for a moment, eyes damp, hand shifting so she could curl her fingers around his. "Yeah. Uh. Well, good," she said then muttered. "Not that you get a say because it's my body and you can just eat your half of the burrito and keep your opinions to yourself."

"I shouldn't have said that before—well, I shouldn't have said a lot of things, but in this case, I meant about your dress." He sighed. "I spent lots of time saying that you were pushing me away, but I did just as good of a job of shoving you away in return."

Silence as she studied him.

Then, "Yes." A murmur. "You did." A squeeze of his hand before pulling back and picking up her burrito. "But don't beat yourself up about it. We both made mistakes."

Mistakes.

Fuck. He'd made so many.

Including, leaving her alone in a restaurant to be pitied and stood up and—

"You okay?"

Jet nodded.

"You sure?"

He picked up the burrito, but his stomach was churning and so he promptly set it down again.

He needed to tell her about the date.

He should have already done so.

Fuck. So. Many. Fuck-ups.

By this point, Trix had some food in her belly, but not enough wine in her bloodstream. Which meant her stomach was happy, her mind was in top form, and thus, she was paying attention.

And knew he was being really fucking weird.

"Jet."

More booze. Yes, that was the solution.

He picked up the bottle to top off her glass.

He'd wait until she finished her wine and mellowed out and then confess—

She hopped out of her chair, which made every muscle in his body stiffen, but instead of moving toward the door, like he'd half-expected, Trix moved around the island, took the wine from his hand and set it down, then plunked herself into his lap.

Now he had the creamy skin of her breasts nearly at eye level, her bare thighs splayed across his lap.

He made a sound that was half-groan, half-pleasure, but somehow kept his hands at his sides. She hadn't invited him to touch and—

Her palm rested on his chest, the other rose to cup his cheek and tilt his face up. "Spill," she ordered. "Now."

Coconut. Flowers.

Curves.

Exposed skin.

His mind couldn't focus on her words with all of those distractions in front of him.

"*Jet.*"

"I'm the reason you were stood up tonight," he blurted, totally tactlessly, completely opposite to how he'd planned to break the news to her.

"*What?*"

And the blurting continued. "I asked Heather to set up the date but only with you. Not with Monroe. I was going to meet you there, to show up instead of Monroe, and to . . . I don't know, swoop in and save the day."

Gray eyes fixed onto his. "Please, tell me you're kidding."

He winced at her tone. "I'd planned to come in after Heather texted me, but then Heather *never* texted me, and at first you didn't reply. But then you said you were leaving and had mentioned the taqueria and—"

Her body was actually vibrating with fury.

He grabbed her hips to steady her.

"You—" She gasped in a breath. "I—" Another. "How—?"

"I'm sorry," he said. "I don't know what I was thinking. I just wanted a chance to have another date with you, and—"

"Let me get this straight," she said, shifting in his lap and glaring up at him. "You got Heather to set me up on *another* blind date after our first one went so well"—lightning in those gray eyes—"but that date was one that I was supposed to be stood up—"

"I—"

"And then, when you were going to somehow come in and meet me there instead, *you* ended up standing me up instead?"

He winced. "I—"

"And now you try to bribe me with tacos and wine, like that was somehow going to make it all okay?"

Here she stopped talking and just stared at him.

"Um, yes?"

Her body was still vibrating in anger, bouncing on his lap in a way that he was certain she didn't intend. One that felt good and—

He was a total fucking perv.

"I—" A gasp. "Cannot—" One more. "Believe. You."

And then she burst into laughter.

Since that was pretty much the last thing he'd expected, Jet jerked so hard that he almost upset Trix and dumped her from his lap. Luckily, she reached for his shoulders, holding on and dropping her head to his chest.

He could feel her laughter through his shirt, hot, damp puffs of air soaking through the cotton of his button-down.

He was frozen in place, both in shock and scared to move and have the laughter turn back to fury. But then he thought back to her expression, to the sounds she'd made as he'd tried to explain and realized that she'd been laughing at him for much longer than he'd thought.

"You're such an idiot," she said, the words punctuated with giggles.

"I think that has been repeatedly established."

She stilled, face tilting up, eyes warm, lips curved. "You really wanted a date with me that badly?"

"Badly enough to concoct a scheme with Heather and make utter fools of both of us?" She nodded and there was no point in denying anything. "Yes."

"Idiot," Trix repeated.

"Yes," he said again.

Then she surprised him again.

Shifting in his lap, she stretched up and pressed her mouth to his.

FIFTEEN

Trix

A PLETHORA OF EMOTIONS. Too many damned feelings.

And all she wanted was her mouth against Jet's.

So . . . she kissed him.

The moment their lips touched, heat exploded throughout her body. Shooting south from her mouth, down her nape, her chest, her nipples beading against the fabric of her dress. It expanded in her stomach, arrowed between her thighs and—

He tore his lips from hers.

"Trix—"

She shifted in his lap, leaning back enough to slip one leg over to the other side, to straddle him. Of course, that meant he got a full view of what she was wearing under her dress . . . which wasn't much.

His eyes told her he liked the skimpy black cotton.

"Talk later," she murmured, shimmying close enough that her breasts brushed his chest so that she could reach up and weave her hands into his hair. "Fuck now."

Chocolate eyes went liquid, like hot fudge, and she shivered, thinking that particular fantasy was definitely moving to the top of her list.

Jet's lips were very close to hers. "What just went through your mind?"

She told him.

His hips shifted beneath hers, jerking up restlessly, and telling her all she needed to know about what he thought of that.

"Is that a yes?" she murmured.

"To the hot fudge?" he asked. "Or the fucking?"

"Either. Both." She grinned. "But how about just the fucking today? We need to stock up on supplies."

His expression was serious. "Are you sure, sweetheart?"

Her heart skipped a beat. "Yes, love," she murmured. "I don't think there's been a day when I *haven't* wanted you. Even when I hated you, I wanted you."

"Fuck, Trix. I'm so sorry." Regret chased desire from his face.

That hadn't been her intention, pulling him out of this moment, throwing the past in his face. "No," she murmured. "I didn't mean it like that."

He cupped her cheek. "You'd be better off finding someone else."

"Then I would continue to have this giant hole in my heart where you belong."

His lips parted, breath coming out on a long, slow exhale. "Baby," he murmured. "I'm—"

"Going to kiss me now," she interrupted, "and give me multiple orgasms because we're moving on from the past and going to see if whatever it is between us has a future." A shaky breath and she put all of that growth and effort to good use.

She'd spent months and years finding the strength to shed her armor, and now she was going to let it fall at Jet's feet. "Because I don't want to have this hole inside me anymore. I want you there instead."

His forehead dropped, resting against hers. "How did you get to be so smart?"

She inhaled his scent, the spice comforting and familiar and . . . home. "Probably because I got that 526 on the MCATs."

He laughed.

She laughed.

And then his mouth stole hers, swallowing her giggles, replacing them with his tongue as he kissed and kissed and kissed her.

There was absolutely nothing like Jet's mouth, his lips firm against hers, moving in tandem but never rough, always on the right side of demanding, of coaxing her to not get lost in the moment but to be an active participant. His tongue flicked and teased, then drew back, encouraging hers to move forward, to tangle with his in his mouth. Back and forth they went, mouths meeting, lips melding until Trix was so hot and riddled with desire that she was surprised she didn't turn into a puddle of goo and slide off Jet's lap onto the floor.

He released her mouth, allowing her to suck in some much-needed oxygen and not transform into that puddle on the floor. His lips moved down along her throat, nipping at her collar-bones. "Last chance, babe."

"I never had any chance when it came to you."

He froze, head coming up, eyes meeting hers. Their gazes locked for a long, pulsing moment before he smiled and said, "Likewise, sweetheart." The warmth in the words, on his face made her heart skip a beat, but then his arms were banding around her again, pulling her close and lifting her as he rotated and got up from the stool. "Up, baby," he coaxed, encouraging her a little higher so she could more easily wrap her legs around his hips.

And then his mouth was on hers and they were moving.

To the wall, to the floor. The couch. The bed.

Trix didn't give a fuck. His lips snapped the last threads of her tentativeness, burned away all of her control.

She needed him. *Now.* So, she told him with her tongue, with her lips, with hips rocking against his waist, her breasts rubbing over his chest, her—

He dropped her onto the bed, immediately following her down, and she was rewarded with the sensation of *all* of his hard body pressing against hers. Lips against hers, one hot, rushed kiss before his mouth ran along her jaw, nipping her earlobe, the spot behind her ear that always sent a shiver down her body.

Jet had forgotten *nothing.*

And he put it all to good use.

Fingers sliding up the outside of one thigh, slipping under the hem of her dress to knead her ass. Mouth moving down, kissing across her chest, nudging the straps out of the way as he moved. Then he reared back, reaching for the fabric covering her breasts, but in her surprise at the backward movement, she missed that he was moving closer, and for one horrible moment, she thought he was going to stop. To leave again.

That feeling faded as soon as she saw his face, but he knew. *He knew.* His eyes gentled, his mouth pressed lightly against hers.

"I'm here," he murmured.

Just *I'm here.*

She wrapped her arms around him, tugging him back down, soaking in the comfort of his warm weight. "I know," she whispered.

One pause. One moment. One remembrance of things gone wrong.

And then time shifted again, the past disappeared back where it belonged, and Trix slid her hands into his hair. Jet shifted enough to take her mouth, one hand braced by her head, the other tracing up and down her side.

When they broke for air, she smiled up at him. "You do know there's a zipper there, don't you?"

"Oh?" His fingers tickled her ribs lightly then gripped the pull, tugged it down. When he glanced up at her, his lips were twitching. "I guess I missed that."

He leaned back, and this time she didn't have that moment of panic.

Because he was reaching for the material, tugging it down her body and tossing it to the floor.

He froze and she felt unaccountably shy as he stared at her.

Then he met her eyes. "You're the most beautiful thing I've ever seen."

Instinct made her scoff.

"The. Most. Beautiful," he repeated.

Tears burned the backs of her eyes, but she blinked them away, touched his cheek. "*Jet.*"

"I will never waste this chance you're giving me."

She sniffed.

He winced then deliberately lightened his tone. "So, how good are my skills if I can make the woman I love cry in bed?"

Woman. I. Love.

She sucked in a breath, lips parting to—

She didn't know, didn't have time to process. Because his mouth was on hers, tongue sliding home, kissing her until her head spun. Only then did he pull away and make his way down to her breasts, taking off and tossing her bra to the side, before massaging them, then licking and nipping and finally sucking one nipple deeply into his mouth.

"Oh, God," she groaned, spine arching, hands gripping his head tightly.

Pleasure spiraled out from that one point, lighting her body on fire, making her limbs restless and heavy all at once. Then he switched sides and the process repeated, only this time it was even more intense because she was already spinning out of control, her desire on knifepoint.

"Jet?" she asked when he began to kiss his way down her stomach.

"Hmm?" He didn't pause what he was doing, and frankly it wasn't like she was going to complain.

"Can you—*ah*—" He nipped her hip.

"What, baby?"

She blinked. Focused. "Can you take off a few more layers?"

He glanced up at her and then his clothes disappeared. Okay, really, he tore his shirt over his head, kicked off his shoes, and leaned back enough to unbutton and kick his pants from his legs.

Meanwhile, she got to enjoy the show.

Jet wasn't bulky in any sense of the form, but he had a lean strength that made her fingers itch with the desire to trail them over his chest, to drift down the flat planes of his stomach, to slip under the waistband of his boxer briefs and—

He gently knocked her hands away when she reached for him. "Next time," he murmured and continued kissing his way down her stomach, tugging her underwear down. It flew off somewhere, but she was much less focused on where it landed because his slightly roughened palms were coaxing her thighs apart, trailing up the insides, one finger sliding through the wet heat of her pussy.

Then he bent and replaced his finger with his mouth.

And it was absolutely everything.

Her nerves had slowly been winding tighter and tighter as he'd kissed his way down her body, and by the time his tongue slid up through her folds and his mouth latched onto her clit, she was nearly nonsensical.

More. Need. Pressure. Harder.

Separate thoughts punctuated with gasps and moans, and Jet went down on her like he'd never forgotten a single thing about what she liked, what sent her spinning, what made her cry out in pleasure.

"Oh fuck, Jet!"

"Mmm." His groan vibrated against her clit, ratcheting her higher . . . until the next flick of his tongue sent her plummeting over the edge.

She groaned, head pressing back against the pillow, hips jerking, and pleasure burning through her.

"Fuck," she murmured.

Jet slowed his movements, softening his tongue, easing her through to the other side.

He crawled up next to her, tugging her close, holding her tightly against his chest. His cock was hard against her side, but he didn't press it closer, didn't arch against her, and she knew he wasn't going to make the next move. This was her show and for the most part, he was letting her call the shots.

"Have I mentioned that sometimes a girl just likes to be dominated in bed?"

Silence.

Then he slowly propped himself up on one elbow and bent so he could see her face. At her expression, one brown brow lifted.

"Is that so?"

She spun in his hold, resting one hand on his chest, feeling the light sheen of sweat beneath her palm. "Sometimes a woman just wants her man to flip her over and fuck her into oblivion."

His hands clenched on her hips, but his tone was light. "Oh? Do you know any men who might be up for that?"

Trix tapped a finger against her lips. "In this bed?" she asked innocently. "I don't think so—"

Her teasing cut off on a shriek when Jet lifted and threw her back onto the mattress. His hands were everywhere, cupping, teasing, sliding, and generally driving her insane . . . or at least, back up to the precipice. And he wasn't even inside her yet.

Head thrashing on the pillows, she moaned, "I need—"

"Hush." He nipped at her bottom lip. "I know what you need." And then he slipped a finger inside her, thumb pressing against her clit, arrowing pleasure through her body. In mere minutes she went from sated to writhing with need.

Up and up she went, climbing that mountain, muscles locking, heat blasting through her. She thought that Jet would slow, would pull back and reach for a condom, but he didn't. Instead, he kept working her, not pausing, not giving in, even when she gasped that it was, "Too much."

He just slipped another finger inside, circled his thumb more firmly, and . . . she catapulted over the edge.

That was when he reached for his nightstand, grabbed a condom, and rolled it down his cock. Then he was lifting one of her legs up, wrapping it around his waist, and sliding home.

So. Fucking. Good.

He paused, glanced down at her, and she would swear the smile he gave her brought her halfway to another orgasm all on its own.

Then he was moving, and she was wrapping her other leg

around his waist, and they were as close as two people could be —sharing bodies, sharing breath, sharing . . . ecstasy.

He groaned, head dropping to her shoulder while she cried out again, somehow finding more pleasure, but also feeling absolutely certain that being held in Jet's arms was the only place she'd wanted to be.

Forever.

SIXTEEN

Jet

HE WAITED until Trix was out before carefully slipping from the bed and heading back to the kitchen. It only took a few minutes to pack up the remains from their dinner, and it was probably a fruitless effort since they wouldn't be very good reheated anyway. But his fridge was pretty sparse, and unless she wanted to subsist on saltines and the rest of the bottle of wine, then a reheated taco was the best he could do.

"Hey."

His eyes shot from the fridge to where Trix had come out of the bedroom, one of his T-shirts slipped over her head, vulnerability written across her face.

"Hey, sweetheart," he murmured, closing the fridge and heading over to her. He wrapped an arm around her waist, tugged her close. "I was trying to salvage dinner."

The hesitation disappeared from her eyes. "I think that might be impossible."

"Probably," he agreed then turned her in his arms. "You okay?"

She smiled and nodded. "I had three orgasms, how could I *not* be okay?"

Except, the hesitation was still there, the shadows behind her eyes. She might not be aware of them, or was, perhaps, shoving them down because she didn't want to ruin the moment. The difference between the past and now was he knew that she deserved a partner who wanted to make that slice of uncertainty disappear.

"I'm not going to leave," he murmured. "I know it will take time for you to trust me, but . . . I'm not cutting ties ever again."

"Jet—"

He laid a finger on her lips. "If things end up not working for us, and I hope to God that isn't the case because you're the one woman I've had in my life that has meant enough for me to push beyond my past then at the very least, I don't want to lose you as a friend." He brushed his finger lightly back and forth. "You were the best one I ever had."

She sucked in a breath, her mouth moving against his finger as she pressed a kiss there. "What happened that made it so hard? I mean, I know your parents weren't great, but why—"

And there was the crux of it. He'd told her a little, but not enough.

Without warning, Jet scooped her up into his arms and carried her back to his bed. Only this time, he didn't drop her on the mattress and make love to her. Instead this time, he set her down, reclined beside her, and proceeded to tell her all of the fucked-up shit from his childhood.

"My parents had money," he said. "Like yours. And like yours, there were strings. At first, it was typical stuff. I could have the new bike if I got all As or the new video game or the new whatever was popular with my friends at the time." She nodded when he glanced down at her. "A lot of my friends were in similar situations. Buying affection and obedience with things, that's not out of the ordinary. Neither was me hardly seeing them."

Clarity began to shine in her eyes.

"My dad worked a lot. Typical. My mom was busy at the club and with whatever charity business or other things that kept her occupied. I was raised by nannies. Whatever, lots of people do that." He shrugged. "It's sometimes the only way."

"But?" she prompted when he hesitated.

"But, I can count on two hands the number of times I remember seeing my parents growing up. I'm sure it was more, that they were there and I just don't remember." He sighed. "But I do remember begging them to be there for my fifth birthday and Christmas"—he had been born on the 27th—"but them saying that fell during their trip to Vail, and I shouldn't inconvenience them. I remember that happening again for several years and getting the same answer." Jet shook his head. "Then asking to go with them to Vail. I'm guessing you know their answer already?"

She bit her lip and nodded. "I think I do."

"Yeah, it was a no," he said. "And a no to Father's and Mother's Day. A no to the presents I made them in school. I remember coming home so excited to give my mom a frame I'd made in class, some ugly thing made of popsicle sticks and paper flowers. My mom accepted it, but when I hugged her, she shoved me away and said I was wrinkling her outfit." A sigh. "And then I found the frame in the trash the next day."

Trix's eyes were glassy with tears. "Oh, Jet, I'm—"

"I'm not telling you this because I want you to feel bad for me," he said quickly. "I know it was fucked up, and I know I was an innocent kid who didn't deserve to be pushed away and emotionally abused and . . . frankly, neglected in a lot of ways. That wasn't right."

"No, it wasn't."

"It took me a long time to understand that and to come to terms with a lot of my life choices. My father wanted me in the family business, hated when I'd gone premed, but because it was a respectable profession, he'd allowed me to continue on." He rolled his eyes. "I should have gone my own way then, but instead, I kept trying, kept almost begging for the scraps of affection. I expected pride when I graduated as valedictorian, approval for getting into med school, and I never got any. Then they died in the accident and—"

He sucked in a breath, not wanting to say the words aloud, but Trix just put her palm on his chest and waited.

"And part of me was happy about it."

Her face didn't change. She didn't pull away. "I call that normal, Jet."

"Maybe," he said. "But I didn't understand it at the time. I felt so fucking guilty and horrible that I walled myself off. I would never let myself care about people like that, let people in who would disappoint and hurt me." He met her eyes. "They would be the ones begging for bits of affection. Not me. *Never me*."

She wrapped her arms around him. "And then me. *Us*."

"Yes," he said. "I didn't want to care, and then I couldn't help myself."

"And I was just as closed down, or at least I made a good show of acting like it."

"Yeah."

"So you cared too much and panicked."

He nodded. "Yes."

Trix shifted, touching her forehead to his. "And what's going to stop you from panicking now?"

Maybe once that would have pushed him away, made him freeze up and back away and be a real fucking idiot. But he knew what he was risking if he went down that road now.

And he wasn't going to lose Trix.

Not ever again.

"Because I love you," he murmured. "Because I did then and I do now, and I understand how precious and wonderful and special that is. I won't risk you, baby. Not when you mean so much."

Her eyes were wide, and no words came.

"Are you freaking out?"

She nodded.

"Are you going to run?"

She was silent for long enough that his intestines practically tied themselves into knots. But then she shook her head. "No, baby," she murmured.

"Okay."

Teeth pressing into a plump pink lip. "Okay."

"I'm going to show you that I mean what I say."

"Okay," she said again.

"And stop talking so you have some time to process."

"Okay."

"And—"

"Jet?"

"Yeah, honey?"

She nuzzled into his chest. "Stop talking and just hold me."

He grinned. "Okay, sweetheart."

"And stop saying *okay*."

"Okay."

Her head popped up, eyes narrowed. "*Jet*."

"*Trix*."

She dropped back down. "Night."

"Night, baby."

He tugged the covers up and held her while she drifted off to sleep, content that they had this second chance, that he'd laid it all on the table, that she understood and could forgive him enough to move forward.

He let his eyes slide closed, knowing that this was his future and it was going to be great.

And then he woke with empty arms.

Empty *fucking* arms.

SEVENTEEN

Trix

SHE WAS FREAKING OUT.

It was just after four-thirty in the morning, she was freaking out, and . . . she was doing a strange impersonation of a walk of shame in Jet's shorts, a T-shirt, and a pair of socks she was going to throw out the minute she got back to his place.

One, she needed to check on her car and make sure it was still there.

She couldn't remember if the street parking she'd pulled into had allowed for overnight parking.

Number two, she needed shoes that were not stilettos.

And clothes that fit.

Luckily, she had a go bag in the back of her car with extra sneakers and a change of clothes.

If her car was still there.

She rounded the corner, gut twisting, almost expecting to see an empty spot, but no, her little hybrid was still there.

Thank God.

She hurried over to the trunk and pulled out her duffle,

sitting on the bumper and peeling off the socks before swapping them for the pair in the bag, then slipping on her shoes. She was still in Jet's shorts and shirt, but a wardrobe change would have to wait for his condo. San Francisco streets did see a lot, but one thing they *wouldn't* see was her bare ass as she attempted to shimmy into some leggings.

Though . . . maybe Jet would like to see that.

Her smile was huge as she closed the trunk and stepped onto the sidewalk. Molly's was just a few shop fronts down, and it would open in—she pulled out her phone to check the time— less than fifteen minutes.

Great. She'd wait until then.

Grab coffee and some pastries then bring them back up to Jet. He'd certainly earned them.

She grinned again, probably looking like an idiot, but then again, the look matched her outfit. Last night had been . . . well, more than she'd ever hoped. Oh, she was still kind of pissed about the "blind date" Heather and Jet had conspired on, but she was also strangely touched that they'd gone to such lengths to convince her to give Jet another chance.

And then what he'd shared.

How he'd told her he loved her.

How desperately she'd wanted to say it back.

But by the time she'd gotten the courage, he'd fallen asleep, and after the long, emotional night, she hadn't wanted to wake him.

Well, tough. If he wasn't up by the time she got back, then he was getting shaken awake, coffee and pastries thrust in his face, and a declaration of love shouted into his ear.

Okay, maybe not shouted.

Whispered? Murmured? Spoken?

Ah, yes. Spoken.

That was the one.

Another grin, laughter bubbling inside of her. She'd never felt this hopeful, this happy, not even when they'd been together before. It was like the past had shed its heavy scales and now they could both move forward, lighter and free of its restrictions. "Oh lord," she muttered. "I'm way too poetic at five in the—"

She was so focused on her inner monologue, on watching the lights turn on one-by-one inside Molly's and the imminent deliciousness that was about to fill her belly that she didn't notice the footsteps until it was too late.

But she noticed the pain.

A sharp jab of agony across her skull, burning in her knees and palms as they scraped against the pavement. The snap of a bone breaking as her cell was ripped from her hand and her duffle yanked down her shoulder.

Finally, a raging hot slice of pain through her brain when the foot made contact with her head.

Then she felt nothing.

Blackness swept her under.

EIGHTEEN

Jet

HE WAS ALONE, and she wasn't coming back.

It felt like shit to be on this end of that gesture.

And thanks, karma, for granting him the opportunity to feel this horrible.

His cell rang, and he scrambled to grab it off the counter, hoping against hope that it was Trix, but after calling her cell six times and texting more than ten over the last hour since he'd woken, he already knew it wouldn't be.

It was the hospital, and even though he'd known it wasn't Trix, Jet still couldn't bite back the disappointment.

"Hello?" he answered, instead of chucking his phone across the room, like he really wanted to do.

"Can you fill in for me today?" Matt, or Dr. Harding, asked.

Not like he had anything better to do.

"Sure," he said, focusing on something besides the misery he felt. "Is everything okay?" Matt was solid and reliable but had a couple of young kids, one of whom had been pretty sick the previous week.

"Fine," Matt said and coughed. "Except the little germ machine has infected me with some horribly disgusting virus. I've got snot dripping out of every orifice."

"Not sure if that's possible," he said.

"It's not," Matt agreed. "But you get my point."

"Yeah." He stood and headed to the bedroom to change. "You on at seven?" It was just after five, but he was awake and might as well head into the hospital now.

"Yes, thanks, Jet," Matt said and broke off with a sniffle. "I owe you one."

"No worries, feel better." He hung up, dressed, and headed to the hospital. At least he had work to distract him from how royally fucked up his life was.

He didn't know if there had been a full moon the night before or if it was just his luck, but the department was absolutely slammed. Every bed was filled and there was a backup from admitting, which meant that patients who needed to go upstairs were taking up room unnecessarily. This happened for a variety of reasons, not the least of which—and also probably the most frustrating—was budgetary. As in, the med surge floor preferred the ED to take the budget hit instead of them and sometimes kept patients waiting until shift change.

The other reason for the packed ED was . . . sometimes shit just got weird in the department.

They'd be dead for hours and then as though everyone had been cued, multiple admits came at the same time.

The job kept him guessing, that was for sure.

And if he wasn't building clinics or treating people in remote parts of the world, then at least he had some excitement in his life. He stopped by the nurse's station, checking in to make sure they were all okay.

They were and he started to leave, but Rosario stopped him.

"Hey, I know you and Trix are close. I've been trying to get a hold of her for a few hours, but I—"

The hairs on his nape stood up, but he was already spinning around, trying to pinpoint exactly what had set his nerves on edge.

There was a commotion at the ambulance doors.

A shout.

Two figures staggered in, one being supported by the other, taking a few steps in through the doors, and then collapsing in a heap.

He ran.

Rosario ran.

The figures were two women. One, a tiny, plump female with a riot of brown curls spilling down her back. She wore a gray polo shirt that was soaked through with blood. Her skin was pale, sweat dripping down her face.

"Wouldn't let me call 9-1-1," she gasped, trying to get her shoulder back under the other female. "Should have—"

Brown hair. Thin. Tall.

He recognized the sneakers first.

Had seen them here. Seen *her* wearing them here.

Trix.

Oh God, it was Trix.

His hands started moving, searching and assessing her body for the injuries before his brain caught up.

A palm weakly grabbed his wrist. "Didn't—"

"Shh," he said. "I've got you."

He lifted her, rushing through the halls and setting her on the first available bed.

"Jet—"

Blood darkened her brown hair and the arm that wasn't gripping his wrist was completely at the wrong angle, bruising on her cheek, her throat. She was—

"Jet."

He glanced down, and gray eyes met his.

"I-I d-didn't l-leave."

He opened his mouth to tell her he knew that—

But then her eyes rolled back, and she stopped breathing.

HE WORKED on Trix until they kicked him out.

Then stayed in the hall until she was rushed up to surgery.

But the only thing that stayed with him after they'd taken her was the long, steady, unbroken beep of the heart monitor.

He'd lost her.

He hadn't, really.

And he'd lost her anyway.

NINETEEN

Trix

PEELING OPEN her eyelids took an immeasurable amount of effort.

But eventually she succeeded, blinking against the dim light as though she hadn't seen anything nearly that bright in a long time.

Her first wincing peek gave her the image of her feet covered by a pale blue blanket that she recognized instantly. Because it was an institutional standard, that tightly woven cotton covering, as was the way it was draped over her—secure but accessible to both change and view the patient underneath.

She closed her eyes and relaxed back into the pillows, trying to assess what was wrong with her body and how she might have ended up there.

Her arm hurt like hell and felt like it was immobilized in either a splint or a cast, her side ached, her head throbbed, and the skin near her hairline felt as though it were pulled tight . . . so stitches, a broken arm, bruised ribs, and maybe a concussion?

Okay, so it could have been worse.

The last thing she remembered was the wonderful night with Jet. Had she been in some sort of accident leaving his place the next day? All she could recall was waking up in his arms, too early but between the sun rising early and her biological alarm clock telling her it was time to head into the hospital . . .

Her breath caught.

She hadn't gone into the hospital.

She'd gone down to her car, to Molly's, and—

Her lungs froze. Someone had hit her from behind, knocking her to the pavement, kicking her in the side. She'd woken on the sidewalk, Molly next to her and frantic, her phone out and already dialing 9-1-1.

She'd refused to let the woman finish the call, had insisted Molly use Trix's car to drive her to the ED. It was only a few minutes away and not only would it have taken the ambulance longer to come, but it would have also been a waste of resources.

She'd reached for her phone to call Jet, but it hadn't been there.

And since she didn't know his number by heart, she'd figured she would get someone to call him for her.

But that was the last clear memory she had.

Now she was here—Trix forced her eyes open for another glance at the room and recognized she was in *her* hospital, only a few floors up from the ED. Molly must have driven her, and clearly, something hadn't gone quite to plan if she'd been admitted for bruised ribs and a mild concussion.

For one, she'd passed out again.

For another, she felt like she'd been run over by a Mack Truck.

Her eyes closed a second time and she sucked in a slow, shallow breath. As she became more fully awake, her pain level was increasing. She was tough, but it was already getting to unbearable levels.

"Hey."

A cool hand on her forehead.

She peeled back her lids, saw that Jet was there, pale, stubble covering his face, dark circles beneath his eyes. "Trix?" he asked hoarsely.

She started to nod, stopped when it made her pain ramp. "Jet."

Her voice was raspy. Admitted as well as been intubated.

"You hurting?"

"Yeah," she rasped.

"Here." He pushed the button on the line woven around the handle of the bed. She knew it was filled with a sensor that would administer pain medicine immediately.

"You scared me, baby," he murmured after the drugs had hit her veins, taking the edge off her pain. "But I'm glad you're awake."

She reached for his hand. "I didn't leave—" Her words cut off on a wince.

"It's okay," he said. "Don't try to talk. I know you didn't leave me. You were intubated." He brushed his knuckles lightly over her cheek. "I won't say I wasn't heartbroken there for a minute, but that quickly transformed into terrified when they wouldn't let me work on you."

Her eyes widened.

He nodded. "Dr. Joyce called and asked me to fill in. I was here when Molly brought you in—"

"I remember," she whispered in deference to her aching throat, his words sparking her memories. They had stumbled their way inside, Jet had picked her up, and—

"I'm sorry," she said. "I tried to call to warn—"

"You just spent eight hours on an operating table as the doctors worked to control bleeding in your abdomen. That, after coding twice in the ED and not regaining consciousness for three days, and you're worried about whether you tried to call me?"

Oh. So *that's* why she felt like shit.

"I guess," she murmured.

His eyes rolled to the ceiling and he cupped her cheek. "*Baby.*"

"I didn't get to tell you . . ." Exhaustion was creeping up within her as the pain medicine took fully. It weighed her limbs down, made her brain fuzzy.

"It's okay, sweetheart," he said softly. "Sleep now, you can tell me later."

"No," she said, wrenching her lips back open. "I have to tell you now."

"Okay." He brushed the hair back from her face. "Tell me what, sweetheart?"

Black was edging into her vision, fatigue sweeping over her. Unconsciousness was coming for her.

"I . . ." Her eyes closed.

"It's okay," he murmured. "Go to sleep. I'll still be here when you wake up."

She opened her eyes a millimeter, met his gaze, and in her final lucid moment, pushed out, "I love you."

Then got to see his face go soft before she passed out.

TWENTY

Jet

HE STOOD next to the bed, staring down at the woman he loved more than anything, the woman who had just said she loved him.

And she was unconscious.

Why did that seem absolutely fitting for their relationship?

Smiling, he shook his head then sat his ass back down in the chair next to her and pulled out his cell to text Heather. She'd been in the room almost the entire time since her plane had landed at the airport, after having flown home from Berlin when she'd heard the Trix had been hurt.

His cell buzzed with a response almost immediately.

Be there in fifteen minutes.

He tapped out a response.

She fell back asleep, but this is a good sign. She'll probably start being up a lot more.

His phone vibrated a few seconds later.

Okay, then I'll wrap up my meeting and come over. Do you think an hour is all right?

He'd all but shooed her away that morning, knowing that Trix wouldn't want her to be behind on her account, not if everything was okay.

I think she'll be happy to see you whenever you can make it in.

A reply a heartbeat later.

I'll be there within the hour.

Jet smiled. Heather really was a good sister.

He pocketed his cell, sat back in the chair, and watched his woman as she slept. Nothing else but Trix mattered at that point, not that the police had spoken with Molly—who'd apparently seen a flash as someone had run by her restaurant and then had seen Trix on the ground. It didn't matter that the detective had come to the hospital, leaving his card, and telling Jet that they were pulling the footage of the attack from Molly's cameras, nor that the person who'd hurt Trix was still on the streets somewhere.

The police were almost certain the attack had been random, based on the amounts of grab and go robberies in the city.

Not that it mattered. In fact, in a way, it was almost worse.

Trix had almost died because some asshole wanted an iPhone . . . and not even a new one.

Now she'd be dealing with potentially life-changing injuries for a very long time, if not permanently. People didn't just bounce back from major surgery, even if those people were as tough as Trix.

She had a long road to recovery ahead of her.

And he wasn't going anywhere.

"I've got it," Trix snapped, clearly done with the amount of hovering that he and Heather were doing.

He recognized that and handed back the bag of popcorn she'd been trying to open. In truth, *struggling* to open. Because she'd been out of the hospital for less than a day and was weak after spending nearly two weeks prone in bed. Now, she'd been walked a little bit—yes, he'd thought that correctly, because Heather had made sure Trix had taken several faltering passes up and down the hall.

So, he got that Trix was two heartbeats away from losing her shit.

Heather, as smart of a businesswoman as she was, missed the cues and promptly snatched the bag of popcorn from Trix's lap, opened it, and poured it into a bowl, which she then handed over. And all the while, she kept talking about the nurse she'd hired against Trix's wishes—the irony of a nurse taking care of another nurse was not lost on him, considering he'd taken a few days off in order to help Trix while she recovered, also against her wishes—as well as the food delivery she'd set up.

The latter Jet wasn't sad about.

The first, he thought was overkill.

But he also knew that Heather's heart was in the right place.

That didn't mean Trix couldn't use a little backup in dealing with the overprotectiveness that was Heather. Plus, it wouldn't do for Trix to reinjure something while trying to throttle her sister.

"Two nurses and a doctor," he said, weaving his arm through Heather's. "That sounds like the title to a bad porno."

Trix's eyes met his as he led Heather to the door.

I got this, he mouthed and watched her shoulders drop in relief.

"I think one nurse and one doctor have got this," he went on. "Thanks for the gesture, but we're fine. We'll let you know if we end up needing help."

"But—"

He picked up her coat, helped her shrug into it, then opened the door.

"We'll be okay," he assured. "You go on home to your husband. He's missing you."

Heather nibbled at her bottom lip, but he just propped his door slightly ajar, and led her toward the elevator, pushing the button to call it. Thankfully, it opened right away and he . . . well, he basically shoved her inside the car.

"We'll call you," he said as the doors began to shut.

"I—"

She was cut off as they sealed shut.

He was at the condo's door when his phone buzzed.

I'm well aware that I've just been handled.

Jet grinned.

Another buzz.

You're good for her. You love her right.

Yes, he did, he thought as he walked back into his condo and saw her asleep on the couch, the bowl of popcorn untouched, her hair a mess, her sexy body clad in absolutely shapeless pajamas.

And still the prettiest thing he'd ever laid eyes on.

So, yeah, he loved her right.

And he was going to keep on doing it forever.

Two WEEKS LATER, he walked through the door to his condo, hung up his jacket, and turned to see—

The table set.

Candles ready to be lit.

Delicious smells coming from the kitchen.

The woman he loved in a little black dress that made him crazy.

She was barefoot, headphones in, swaying to the music, and finally looking healthy and recovered for the first time since the attack.

God, he loved this woman.

He'd only returned to work a couple of days before, and this week was going to be hell on that front, as he began to make up for all the extra shifts the other docs had covered for him.

Then he'd come home to this.

Pretty, lovely Trix in his place, cooking at his stove, in a sexy dress, and more importantly, healthy and happy.

She spun, startling slightly when she saw him then tugged the headphones from her ears and strode over to him. "They got him," she said, throwing her arms around his neck, and for once the movement wasn't carefully calculated or punctuated with a wince.

"Got who?"

"Him," she said again, and then he understood.

"They arrested the guy who hurt you?"

She nodded. "They had his face from Molly's cameras, and they got him."

Jet blew out a relieved breath. "That's fantastic news."

"I know." She pressed a kiss to his cheek. "Also, I gave up the lease on my apartment, and so I'm moving in. And Molly was so excited to hear about the arrest that she brought a bunch of food up. I'm talking pastries and salads and this delicious potato and leek soup. I'm just reheating it along with some bread she baked."

His heart lurched in his chest. "What did you say?"

"That Molly baked bread?" Her head cocked. "That's not news, she does it every day."

"No," he said. "Before that."

Her lips twitched. "That I'm reheating soup?"

He shook his head.

"The pastries and salads and potato and leek soup—"

A roll of his eyes. "Enough about the soup."

"The arrest?"

"*Trix.*"

She smiled at him innocently. "Oh, that I'm moving in?"

He dropped his head, nuzzled her throat. "Mmm-hmm."

A shrug. "I decided I'm keeping you."

"You—" He straightened, happiness expanding in his chest, stealing his ability to speak. Never would he *ever* be able to predict what this woman would say or do. She'd keep him guessing . . .

Forever.

And that was just fine with him.

Because he could surprise her, too.

"As it happens," he murmured, nibbling at her jaw. She melted at his touch, leaning closer, brushing her breasts across his chest. "I found a different roommate, so that's not going to work—"

She gasped, leaning back. "How dare—"

Jet kissed her.

And then scooped her up into his arms and brought her to bed.

Luckily, Trix forgave him for his joke and kissed him back.

They wouldn't get to the food that Molly brought until much later.

But that was just fine with both of them.

TWENTY-ONE

Trix

"THAT'S THE LAST ONE," Heather said from her spot next to Trix at the apartment door. They were supervising the men moving Trix's belongings, cramming them jigsaw-style into the back of their various vehicles.

"Why aren't we paying someone to do this again?" Clay asked with a groan. "You're a billionaire and—"

Heather pinched his butt as he walked by.

Clay jumped but kept moving, though she thought his groan was warranted, considering he'd gotten the box filled with her books. And since she hadn't had much time to collect belongings while abroad, she'd been making up for lost time at the bookstores recently. That bin was filled to the top with romance and mystery and fantasy novels of various sizes.

She'd gotten her money's worth. That was for sure.

"Because manual labor is good for your abs," Heather said without missing a beat.

Clay gasped and whipped around. "Are you saying my abs are getting soft?"

"I'm saying that I love your abs," Heather said sweetly, turning to Trix with a wicked smile. "And I want it to stay that way."

Clay gaped for a heartbeat then tossed the box into the back of Trix's car and hauled ass over to them, not missing a step as he hauled Heather up into his arms and then proceeded to kiss the sass right out of her.

Jet grinned as he walked much more slowly over to Trix and slung an arm over her shoulders, leading them both away from the couple making out and into the apartment that had been home.

Her first ever real home.

Or maybe that wasn't right.

Maybe home had always been Jet.

"Do you know," she said when they wandered into the empty kitchen, "the reason that I rented this place?"

He stopped, glanced over at her.

This was the first time he'd ever been in the apartment.

She took his hand, led him to the window, positioning him exactly so he could see what she'd seen when she'd initially viewed the place.

Trix knew the moment he realized it. His shoulders jerked, head whipping around to face her. "That's—" He broke off, shook his head. "I don't—"

"I know," she murmured.

She'd felt a little bit speechless the first time she'd seen it.

It being the view of the hills in the distance, their tops dusted with pale brown, the fog crawling toward them, the ocean to one side, the spiked white tops of boats on the Bay on the other.

Just like *their* place.

Where they'd fallen in love.

On the coast of Africa, they'd stayed slightly inland at a

small village surrounded by hills, a view of the ocean in the distance and a small inlet on the other side. There had been masts there, too, though not quite as tall and definitely not as modern.

But it was close enough to *their* place that she'd felt a sharp pang upon seeing it.

Then hadn't been able to imagine living anywhere else.

She'd pretended it was cheaper because that was easier than admitting she'd never stopped loving Jet, never stopped thinking about him or wishing that things would have turned out differently.

And now he realized that, too.

"Baby," he murmured, turning to face her and cupping her cheek in his palm. "This is—"

She covered his palm with her own. "We've talked a lot over the last few weeks, shared a lot about what makes us tick. We'll, *you've* shared," she added. "I've only yelled at you about what our relationship had meant to me."

"That's not true—" he began.

"It's true." She sighed. "I've shared bits and pieces, yes, but I don't think I ever explained to you why I was so closed down, why it's hard for me even now thinking about telling you, why I was scared to accept *anyone* fully into my life—whether it was you or Heather or friends or lovers."

He tugged her against his chest. "It's not an easy thing to lay yourself bare," he murmured. "And I can afford to be patient while you get comfortable."

"And was it easy for you to share?"

A chuckle that vibrated against her ear. "Hell, no. I still have to fight against the urge to keep everything as some sort of joke, to tuck all of those insecurities away, to not pretend my past didn't affect me."

Trix leaned back slightly. "I don't have a horrible neglect story like you."

He snorted. "Thanks."

Her heart twisted. "I didn't mean it like that—"

"I know, babe," he said. "There's me trying to lighten it."

"You're saying we should embrace our dark senses of humor?"

"I'm saying there's no other way."

She sighed, letting her forehead move forward to bump against his collarbone. "I felt alone a lot as a kid."

His arms tightened, chin tilting to rest on the top of her head, but he didn't say anything, just waited for her to gather her thoughts . . . or maybe for her to signal that now wasn't the time.

But Trix had realized that life was too fucking short for this to *not* be the time.

This was it.

She didn't want any more barriers between them.

She didn't want any more barriers between herself and the people who meant something in her life.

She wanted everything out in the open, the secrets that pressed so heavily down on her chest gone, their power reduced to ashes, whatever shameful hold they'd had on her for so long gone.

Trix was done being tied down by the past.

Lifting her head, she glanced over Jet's shoulder. "You might as well come in, too, Heather. You should hear this."

Heather, whose blonde hair had been peeking around the corner as she shamelessly spied on Trix and Jet, startled and jumped back. "I'm just—"

"Nosy," Trix said and smiled to soften the word. "But I know that it comes from caring about me." She turned in the circle of

Jet's arms, held out her hand. "I didn't trust that for a long time, but when I finally realized the life I was living didn't make me happy, and I wanted to come home . . . where did I come?"

"California."

"No," Trix murmured. "To you." She smiled. "You were the one person who proved to me time and again that you actually gave a shit about me."

Heather's eyes went damp. "Come here." She took Trix's outstretched hand and tugged her from Jet's arms, wrapping her in a tight hug.

"You never stopped reaching out," Trix murmured. "Even when it pissed me off, when I was trying to get far away from here and forget everything that had happened, you always managed to track me down." She sniffed, blinking back tears. "I was so thankful for that . . . even when it was really fucking annoying."

They both laughed and held on to each other for a long moment.

"I am good at being annoying," Heather deadpanned and pulled back after they'd both chuckled.

"I never thought I was good enough," Trix said.

Heather's face sobered. "Trix—"

"No," she said. "Let me get this out?"

Heather nodded.

But she didn't really know where to start. How could she possibly begin to explain the black hole that had been inside her, the bottomless pit that sucked in every single good thing inside of her, making it disappear, leaving her empty and fragile and . . . not good?

How could she begin to put *that* into words?

She turned and glanced at Jet. His eyes were calm, his arms extended, his expression patient. "You're worth the time, baby. This doesn't have to happen today. But your pain is *your* pain.

You don't have to justify it. You're *allowed* to feel what you feel, no explanations required."

Her heart rolled over in her chest. "God, I love you."

His lips twitched at the corners. "I know."

She crossed to him, let him wrap his arms around her, and then she started talking.

She told them about being the *other* family, about her mother spending all the money, about living on a loaf of bread and a jar of peanut butter for two weeks—those being her mother's rations. She told them about mowing the neighbor's lawns and cobbling her piggy bank with her brothers' to pay the water bill while their mother came home with a new handbag or a pair of Louboutins. She told them about all the screaming, the way her brothers had left home as soon as they were able, and how she'd hated them for doing so, even while understanding their need to escape.

She shared how she'd gone to her father and asked for money to pay the power bill at fourteen.

And how he'd told her that her mother had already pestered him for child support for four kids he didn't even want.

She confessed about her mother's drinking. The hateful words that followed.

Finally, she told them about med school, not qualifying for loans because she had no credit and the market had crashed, because her parents made too much, because she'd spent every cent she earned putting herself through undergrad.

"He refused to pay," Trix said. "Refused even to sign a contract that it would be a loan, that I would pay back every cent. He said making a crew of useless Donovans was the absolute worst thing he'd ever done in his life, and *that* was why he'd refused to give us his name."

Jet had stiffened behind her throughout the monologue, but

his touch when he spun her in his hold and stared down at her face was as gentle as someone handling fragile crystal.

"I'm okay," she said, touching his cheek.

"Nothing about this is okay."

"I don't want his name," she murmured. "I never did. I just wanted a place where I belonged."

"You belong," he said. "Here. With me."

"And me," Heather said, voice watery. "I'm sorry. I didn't know—"

"How *could* you?" Trix said. "You were away at school, and it wasn't like I reached out . . . or even knew how. Our father is excellent at separating people."

Heather's gaze dropped to the floor. "Yes, he is." She sucked in a breath. "I just wish . . ."

"That things could be different."

Heather nodded.

"I know, me, too," she said. "But when I finished my last assignment and decided to come home—to come *here*—I didn't know what would become of it. I just knew that I wanted to find a family . . . and that I hoped the family would include you."

Heather closed the distance between them. "Our father is the absolute worst kind of asshole, but I didn't—I mean, I didn't go through what you did. We had money, fucking ridiculous heaps of it. I wish—fuck, I wish I knew that you were struggling. I could have—"

Trix stepped out of Jet's hold and took Heather's hands. "I don't blame you. I never have. Never."

"You should."

"*No.*" She tightened her hold. "I shouldn't. I never have, and I never will. This was never about some sort of you-had-and-I-didn't. This was me putting up walls to survive and then not realizing or being too scared to reach over the top for help.

That's what's changed for me. With you. With Jet. I'm not scared anymore."

Jet gently squeezed her nape. "I know, baby."

Heather gave her a watery smile. "Thank you, Trix. For saying that. I . . . I guess I never felt like my pain could mean anything. I wasn't abused. Yes, he was absent. Yes, he's never praised or told me he loved me. Yes, he was all about the business to the detriment of everything else—"

"That's abuse," Clay interjected, wrapping an arm around Heather's waist. "I'm sorry, I know this isn't my conversation to jump into, but, sweetheart"—he glanced down at his wife —"abuse comes in all forms. Just because he didn't leave physical bruises doesn't mean you don't have emotional ones."

Heather and Trix stilled, and Trix knew her sister was feeling the same pulse of shock that Clay had managed to reduce their feelings down to such a perfect explanation.

Face softening, Heather turned to her husband. "How'd you get so smart?"

"When you married me," he said without missing a beat then chuckled when she lightly smacked him across the chest. "Come on," he said. "Let's leave these two alone and take the first load to Jet's place."

Heather nodded, slipped out of his hold. "Just one more thing."

She came back over to Trix and pulled her in for one more hug, murmuring softly into her ear, "I know our father is really good at using our weaknesses to keep people apart. I also know I spent too long trying to find a reason for what could possibly motivate him to do such a thing." She sighed. "And I came to the conclusion that I'll never understand it. *Never.* I just know that I want *my* family to be different . . . and I really want you to be part of it."

Trix squeezed her lightly. "Well, good. Because you're stuck with me."

Heather dropped her arms, grinning. "I'm glad." A beat and she visibly exhaled the heavy moment from her features. "Now, don't forget to christen the kitchen counters before you lock up. Might as well make the most of your last day here."

Trix retched. "You know, I think that sisters are supposed to be grossed out by their siblings' sex lives."

"I've learned much in my years . . . and one of the most important is that a good orgasm can cure most ills."

Jet wrapped both of his arms around Trix's waist and rested his chin on her shoulder. "Bye, Heather."

"See you soon," she called, heading for the door. "Just not *too* soon."

The door closed behind her.

"You okay?" Jet asked.

Trix rotated in the circle of his arms. "I'm . . . not fine exactly, but I have you. I have Heather, and so that's a damned good start as far as I'm concerned."

"I agree."

"You would—*eek!*" Her hands fell to his shoulders when he swept her up and held her against his chest. "Jet! What are you doing?"

He spun, set her on the counter. "Taking Heather's advice."

"What?" Her brows drew down.

"We're christening these countertops."

"Um. No. That's not going to hap—"

"I love you," he said.

She shook her head. "I love you, but that doesn't mean we're going—"

He cut off her protest with a kiss.

And frankly, it didn't take much more convincing than that for her to play her part in christening those countertops.

Plus, Heather was right.

A good orgasm did cure most ills.

It also helped remove the hooks of the past and tuck it firmly back where it belonged.

So, Trix could focus on the future.

Exactly as it should be.

EPILOGUE

Jet, Six Months Later

HE WALKED into the restaurant five minutes late, eyes searching the area near the hostess stand for Trix.

He'd gotten stuck at the hospital, wanting to wait until a patient was admitted upstairs, and then running home to change because he wasn't going to meet his woman in dirty scrubs.

When he didn't spot her, he frowned. She'd left a note at the condo saying she was running an errand. It had probably just taken her a little longer than she'd expected. He'd sit down, order her a glass of wine, and wait.

He went up to the hostess and asked for his table. Five minutes later, he had drinks on the table and an untouched bread basket in front of him.

Ten minutes after that she still hadn't shown.

A little worried now, he sent her a text.

Five minutes after *that*, she still hadn't responded.

Knowing that she probably just hadn't heard the chime, but

his stomach churning anyway—because the last time she'd gone out of contact and it hadn't been because of work was when . . .

She'd been robbed and beaten.

"Fuck," he muttered, not giving a damn that he was in a fancy French restaurant and that it was impolite, he hit her number in his phone and brought it to his ear. It rang four times then went to voicemail.

His gut was churning now.

The server came over, a male in his twenties with a knowing look on his face.

Probably thought that Jet had gotten stood up.

And, he guessed in a way he *had*.

But that thought—Trix having gotten so wrapped up in her errand that she'd forgotten about dinner—was a much better one than her unconscious and bleeding out on the street.

"Would you like to order, sir?"

Jet shook his head. "No. I need the check. Thanks."

"Certainly." A nod. "Might I suggest you try some bread before you go?" He nudged the basket closer. That was weird, but the waiter disappeared before Jet could make heads or tails of the comment.

While he waited for his bill, Jet sent another text.

Still no response.

He pulled out his wallet, intending to just leave cash on the table, when the waiter came back, check in hand and handed it over.

"Did you try the bread?" the server asked.

For fuck's sake.

What the hell was the man's issue with the bread? Was it filled with fucking gold or something? His girlfriend might be out there hurt and—

The man nudged the basket, so it was almost on Jet's plate.

Was he fucking serious?

Jet glanced up, eyes probably sparking fire, a fistful of cash in one hand, and saw the waiter nod encouragingly.

To stop the insanity, Jet grabbed a fucking roll.

And froze.

A little black box sat underneath it.

His heart skipped a beat, the worry settled, and he reached for the box, a neatly folded square of paper taped to the top. He snagged it and at the same time, felt the server gently pry the cash from his other hand—which was mercenary but efficient, Jet supposed—before he was left alone at the table.

The paper shook as he unfolded it.

Will you promise to always share your tacos with me?

He snorted then obliged the arrow that was scrawled beneath the words and flipped the note over.

If so, open the box then come home.
-T

Jet snagged the box and stood, opening it as he strode out of the restaurant, knowing what was inside almost without looking, also knowing that it would go very well with what he'd bought a month before . . . because it was from the same jeweler.

A ring.

He grinned.

Never could predict.

Fuck, he was looking forward to a lifetime of that.

He moved quickly, legs eating up the blocks when his phone rang. He brought it to his ear.

"Hello?"

"So how did it feel?"

"How did *what* feel?" Being briefly terrified for her safety—they would have words about that later—or the ring that meant more to him than anything else ever had? Because she'd given it to him. No strings. No begging. She'd just . . . given.

And that, more than anything, was everything he'd ever dreamed of.

"Getting stood up," she said.

Which was pretty much the last thing he'd been expecting. Again.

The pieces shifted in his mind, coming together, Heather's insistence that she wanted them to go out for a good dinner—one she'd pay for, by the way, so another woman who he was going to have words with later, Trix not specifying her errand, not responding to his texts, his call.

"Oh, man," he muttered. "You play dirty."

He rounded the corner, instinctively knowing she'd be there. Leaning against a pole instead of her car, but phone to her ear, a paper bag of food in her hand.

He hung up, shoved his cell in his pocket, and closed the distance between them.

"You know, we're actually going to have to have a full meal at that restaurant someday," he said, brushing a hand down her cheek.

"I don't know." She shrugged. "Their bread is pretty good."

They laughed and he took the bag as they began walking up to the condo. "I didn't eat it."

She shook her head. "Wasting perfectly good carbs."

They hit the button for the elevator, headed up to their floor. "Looks like you have plenty of carbs in here."

"Had to spring for queso and guac, as per tradition."

He grinned, held the doors as they got off, and walked down the hall.

"So?" she asked when they went inside.

"So what?" he countered innocently.

"Jet!"

He smothered a smile but didn't answer her, instead moving to the hall closet, pulling down the bag he'd stashed there, the one that held an identical box. He turned around, extended it to Trix.

Who crossed her arms.

"I'm not taking it back."

"Good," he said and opened the lid to reveal the diamond ring inside. "Because I'm not taking this one back either."

Those pretty gray eyes dampened, her fingers reached out to touch the band. "You—?"

"Yes," he said when she faltered. "I had a whole day planned. The beach at sunset, a picnic, going down on one knee—"

"You can still do that," she blurted.

Jet grinned, dropping into the position and tugging the ring from the box. He took Trix's hand, slid the metal circle down her finger. "Will you . . . *share your tacos with me?*"

Her face had been soft, but at his words, she gasped and smacked him lightly.

"I love you, baby," he said. "Marry me?"

She dropped to her knees and wrapped her arms around him, lips meeting his, tongues tangling as they kissed and kissed and *kissed*.

When they broke for air, both of them were gasping.

"Is that a yes?" he asked, stroking one finger down her cheek.

"It's a yes," she confirmed, hands starting to undo the buttons of his shirt, mouth pressing to each inch of exposed skin. "To both the marriage thing." A kiss. "*And* the tacos."

He snorted.

She giggled.

And then they made love right there in the hallway.

Which was a good thing because . . . they hadn't christened that spot yet.

EPILOGUE

Molly

SHE CHECKED the bread that was proofing in the oven, not opening the door and risking a disruption of those teeny bubbles that were still forming, but peering through the glass rectangle on the oven and making sure those pale globes of bread were rising as they should.

Her homemade rolls were a top-seller, usually gone before ten in the morning.

That was because they were delicious, if she said so herself.

And she did say so, she supposed, snorting at her pun.

But puns were all she had at zero-dark-thirty in the morning. Zero-dark-thirty otherwise known as four A.M. It was a stupid hour to be up and about, but she owned a bakery and that meant she had to get up early. Molly's—yes, she was egotistical enough to own a place named after herself, though in fairness, she hadn't come up with the name—served breakfast and lunch, with a limited staff and menu for dinner.

That limited menu meant she didn't have to work at dinner time.

A good thing, too. Otherwise, she might as well live at the restaurant.

And while she loved Molly's, she also loved having a life.

Not that you've had much of that lately, she thought.

True.

But owning a restaurant in a big city was difficult, and even more difficult was to *keep* owning it. Molly had investors to reimburse, loans to pay off, wages to cover, and supplies to purchase.

So, that meant filling in if her evening cook had a date or got sick or worked only five days a week. Okay, so if she were being truthful, that meant she all but lived at the bakery an average of four days out of said week.

But that was better than seven, so there was that.

Seeing that the rolls were doing well, Molly turned back to the counter, preparing to finish up the rest of her prep. She had to toast some walnuts, get the mise en place ready for her soups —which was basically a fancy word to say she was chopping up the onions and carrots, celery and potatoes and peppers, measuring stocks and creams, roasting cobs of corn.

Her rolls dinged and she grabbed them out, switching them to the preheated oven, doing a little dance of adding another cookie sheet in to proof, pulling out a tray of croissants that were done from a different oven and replacing them with peach turnovers. She packed up the mise en place and stored them in the fridge, then prepped several bowls of muffin batter—today would be lemon poppy seed, peaches and cream, blueberry, and double chocolate.

Once the turnovers were done, she divided the muffin batter into various tins then began rocking through baking them off while stocking the glass case next to the counter. It was a familiar routine. Her doors opened at five, but that was mostly for her few straggler early birds and that wasn't typically more than five or six people, so she mostly let the first bell tinkling above the door let her know when she needed to pull her ass out of the kitchen. Which meant that she had to have the first batch of everything baked off before that. After her first employees clocked in at five-thirty, she could stay in the kitchen like she preferred.

Baking was her favorite.

The people weren't bad either. She loved getting to know them, to see them change, their lives grow full and happy, their kids get older. She loved *feeding* people, even if they weren't regulars.

There was absolutely nothing better than seeing someone's happy smile when they bit into something tasty.

Speaking of, the bell above the door tinkled as her first customer of the day strode through the door.

"I'll be with you in a second," she called, continuing to fill the case with lemon muffins.

"I did always love to see you like this."

Molly jumped, eyes shooting up.

It had been so long since she'd heard that voice.

I love taking bites out of you.

It had rumbled back then, too, rasping along her skin, skating down her spine, and making her shiver.

The first man she'd baked for.

The man who'd given her the money to open this place.

The one who'd *named* it.

And the one who'd left her at the altar. In the white dress. With the venue booked. With the caterer and the DJ set up. With the guests packing the pews on both sides of the isle.

Jackson Davis.

Jackson *Fucking* Davis.

"Jackson," she murmured and slid the back of the case closed.

"I'm back, honey."

She'd regret her actions later, but in that moment, with the memories of the full church and the people and their pitying expressions and *this man*. Not. Fucking. Showing. Up.

Molly snapped.

She threw the cookie sheet at his head.

BAD WEDDING

Preorder Molly and Jackson's story at www.
books2read.com/BadWedding
Coming July 19th, 2020

BILLIONAIRE'S CLUB

Did you miss any of the other Billionaire's Club books? Check out excerpts from the series below or find the full series at www.amazon.com/gp/product/B07JVRRGCT

———

Bad Night Stand
Book One
www.books2read.com/BadNightStand

Abby

"I'M THE BEST FRIEND," I said and lifted my chin, forcing my words to be matter-of-fact. I'd been through this before. "You might be fuckable to the nth degree and perfect for Seraphina, but I refuse to set her up with a liar."

In a movement too quick for my brain to process, my stool was shoved to the side and I was pinned against the bar, heavy hips pressing into me, a hard chest two inches from my mouth.

Seraphina whipped around at the movement and I could just see her over Jordan's shoulder, her blue eyes concerned.

"Hi, Seraphina, I'm Jordan," he said, calm as can be, gaze locked onto my face then my eyes when mine invariably couldn't stay away. "I'm going to borrow your friend for a minute."

"Abs?" she asked, and I knew she'd go to bat for me right then and there if I needed her to.

"Weasel or no?" I managed to gasp out. For some reason, I couldn't catch my breath.

Not that it had anything to do with Jordan.

No, it had *everything* to do with him.

"Weasel?" he asked.

I shook my head, focused on my best friend. Weasel was our code name for the men trying to weasel, quite literally, their way into my pants and then into hers.

I was just about ready to say fuck it—or me, rather—even if Jordan was a Weasel. He smelled amazing. His body was hard and hot against mine.

And it had been way too long since I'd had sex.

"No chemistry on my part—" Seraphina began.

"Your friend isn't who I'm attracted to," Jordan growled out. "You are, and it's fucking pissing me off that you don't believe that."

Bad Breakup
Book Two
www.books2read.com/BadBreakup

CeCe

"You're even more beautiful than I remember," he said, and the rough edges of his accent hacked at the words, making them more of a growl rather than a soft sentiment.

Her breath caught, and she found her eyes drawn to the stormy blue of Colin's.

And she stared again, utterly entranced before she remembered how it had all ended.

Her in a white dress.

Alone, except for the priest who'd given her a pitying look and invited her to stay as long as she needed.

But it had always been like this, Colin's gruff words winning her over. They were unexpected from him—he was typically so reserved and taciturn. And that compliment, freely given as it was, chipped away at any defenses she managed to erect.

The problem was that his words weren't always followed up by action. In fact, they were typically trailed by pain for her and fury for him.

The hurt of those memories—of Colin so angry, her so broken—helped shore up her resolve.

"Don't say things like that," she snapped and started to pop her earbuds back in. Her friends at home had filled her phone with a slew of romantic audiobooks and she decided that she much preferred fictional heroes at the moment.

At least if they broke their heroine's heart, it was only once.

Colin had already broken hers twice.

She wasn't looking for a round three.

—Get your copy at www.books2read.com/BadBreakup.

Bad Husband

Book Three

www.books2read.com/BadHusband

Heather

"I'm getting drunk," he said, but allowed her to pull him inside the car so that her driver could shut the door behind them.

"You're already drunk," she said.

He stiffened. "*More* drunk."

"Fine," she said, half-worried he was going to launch himself from the sedan. She'd never seen Clay like this. Usually he was so cold and uncompromising, impenetrable even under the toughest of negotiations. He was . . . well, he was typically as *Steele*-like as his last name decreed.

She wrapped her arm through his in order to prevent any unplanned exits from the vehicle and gave the driver the name of her favorite bar. "If you really want to drink, let's do it right."

And *then* she'd drop him at his hotel.

Except it didn't happen that way.

Yes, they hit the bar.

Yes, they drank.

Yes, they got plastered.

But then they woke up . . . or at least, *Heather* woke up.

Naked.

With a softly snoring Clay Steele passed out next to her in bed.

That wasn't the worst part.

Because Heather woke up naked and with a softly snoring Clay Steele in her bed *and* she was wearing a giant diamond ring on her left hand.

Still not the worst part.

That came in the form of a slightly crumpled marriage certificate tucked under her right cheek.

And not the one on her face.

She pulled it from beneath her, a cold sweat breaking out on her body, dread in every nerve and cell.

She *still* wasn't prepared for the horror she found.

The marriage license had been signed by . . . Heather O'Keith and Clay Steele.

Holy fuck, what had she done?

—Get your copy at www.books2read.com/BadHusband.

Bad Hookup
Book Four
www.books2read.com/BadHookup

Rachel

The man didn't take the hint. He didn't leave.

Why won't he leave?

She dropped her chin to her chest.

"So," he finally said after another lengthy—and silent— moment. "Gay, taken, or not interested?"

"Oh my God," she moaned, one hand coming up to push her bangs off her forehead. "This is *not* happening."

"I—" A beat then his voice was incredulous. "I *know* that moan." Warm fingers grasped her wrist, tugged until she could see him in all his yumminess.

Her moment of weakness. Her hookup because she'd been feeling desperate and lonely and—

"It's you," he said softly.

Yes, it was *her*. Rachel, the good girl who didn't sleep around, who *certainly* didn't hook up with random strangers in a bar.

Rachel, who *had* hooked up with a stranger.

The sex had been damned good. Incredible, actually.

But it had been just that. Sex. And she hadn't been able to let go of the guilt. She'd now slept with a grand total of two men in her life, and one of them was her husband.

"I—" She tugged at her wrist. "I need to go."

—Get your copy at books2read.com/BadHookup.

Bad Divorce
Book Five
www.books2read.com/BadDivorce

Bec

Bec really didn't expect to see another person waiting for her when the doors opened with a soft *ding* and she stepped off.

But there *was* another person waiting just outside her front door.

A person she never expected to see again.

Luke Pearson.

Her ex-husband.

It was one-fucking-thirty in the morning, and her ex-husband was sitting on the floor outside her apartment.

Asleep.

Fuming, she marched over to him and kicked his shoe. Hard.

"Luke. Why in the ever loving fuck are you here?"

His lids peeled back and sleepy green eyes met hers. "Becky," he murmured. "You're gorgeous as always." The drowsiness began to fade from his expression. "Did you just come from work?" He glanced down at his phone. "Do you know what time it is?"

"Of course I know what time it is—" Bec bit back the words. Fuck, but wasn't this conversation an exact replica of the broken record one they'd had *way* too many times over the course of their relationship?

She crossed her arms. "Never mind that." A glare that had withered balls much bigger than Luke's "Why did you break into my apartment?"

He stood. "First, I didn't break into your apartment. This is the hall. Second," he hurried to say when she opened her mouth to argue semantics, "I didn't break in. You used our anniversary as the code."

Oh for fuck's sake.

Well, she was changing that tomorrow . . . today . . . fuck, *yesterday*, now that—

"Go away, Luke," she said, pushing past him and unlocking her door while blocking his view of the keypad that was identical to that of the elevator. Her front door's code was not the date of her anniversary with her ex.

But Luke probably already knew that, given that he had been sitting on the floor of her hallway rather than on her couch, beer in hand, feet making prints on her glass coffee table.

Men.

Fucking men.

She slammed the door closed behind her and threw the dead bolt. The knock approximately one second later did not surprise her. Bec dropped her briefcase to the floor then opened it just enough to shoot angry eyes at him through the narrow gap the dead bolt allowed.

Serious green eyes fixed onto hers. "We need to talk."

"Luke," she snapped. "I'm exhausted. It's the middle of the

night. I wouldn't have any patience to talk to my best friends right now, let alone my ex-husband."

"Funny story about that," he said, his lips curving. "Turns out that I'm not actually your *ex*-husband."

—Get your copy at www.books2read.com/BadDivorce

Bad Fiancé
Book Six
www.books2read.com/BadFiance

Seraphina

Sera was alone, pining after a man who'd created the latest social media craze.

Yup. Her life was *ah-maz-ing*.

Tate cleared his throat, and Sera realized she'd been staring at him dumbfounded for a good couple of minutes.

"How can I help you today?" she asked. "I do hope"—*Do hope? What was she, British? Ugh.*—"I-uh . . . I hope you were able to find a house. The agents I passed along are very good at finding unique properties, and I even gave them a few locations to start with . . . " She bit her lip, attempting to stop the ramble.

"No."

Just no.

Um. Okay.

He lifted a hand, rubbed the back of his neck. The movement made his shirt lift, exposing several inches of flat stomach and tan skin and, oh God, a trail of blond hair leading south. Her mouth watered, desperate to trace that path with her tongue—

Sera sucked in a breath, popped to her feet.

"Ah. I'm sorry." She picked up a random file, pretending to know what was in it. "I'm actually really busy, so this will have to continue another time."

Like never.

She rounded her desk, forced a smile. "Mr. Conner," she said when he didn't move. "I'll have my assistant schedule something soon."

"Seraphina."

She shivered at the sound of her name on his lips—soft, a little raspy, and deep enough to conjure all sorts of unhelpful fantasies in her mind.

Shaking herself, she moved to open the door.

Suddenly, Tate was there, hand on hers, body inches away, spicy scent inundating her senses.

Sera's breath caught. "What are you—?"

He seemed to be arguing with himself then finally, those piercing blue eyes locked onto hers. "I need you to marry me."

—Get your copy at www.books2read.com/BadFiance

Bad Boyfriend
Book Seven
www.books2read.com/BadBoyfriendEF

Seraphina

Sera was alone, pining after a man who'd created the latest social media craze.

Yup. Her life was *ah-maz-ing*.

Tate cleared his throat, and Sera realized she'd been staring at him dumbfounded for a good couple of minutes.

"How can I help you today?" she asked. "I do hope"—*Do*

hope? What was she, British? *Ugh.*—"I-uh . . . I hope you were able to find a house. The agents I passed along are very good at finding unique properties, and I even gave them a few locations to start with . . . " She bit her lip, attempting to stop the ramble.

"No."

Just no.

Um. Okay.

He lifted a hand, rubbed the back of his neck. The movement made his shirt lift, exposing several inches of flat stomach and tan skin and, oh God, a trail of blond hair leading south. Her mouth watered, desperate to trace that path with her tongue—

Sera sucked in a breath, popped to her feet.

"Ah. I'm sorry." She picked up a random file, pretending to know what was in it. "I'm actually really busy, so this will have to continue another time."

Like never.

She rounded her desk, forced a smile. "Mr. Conner," she said when he didn't move. "I'll have my assistant schedule something soon."

"Seraphina."

She shivered at the sound of her name on his lips—soft, a little raspy, and deep enough to conjure all sorts of unhelpful fantasies in her mind.

Shaking herself, she moved to open the door.

Suddenly, Tate was there, hand on hers, body inches away, spicy scent inundating her senses.

Sera's breath caught. "What are you—?"

He seemed to be arguing with himself then finally, those piercing blue eyes locked onto hers. "I need you to marry me."

—Get your copy at www.books2read.com/BadBoyfriendEF

Bad Wedding
Book Nine
Coming July 19th, 2020
www.books2read.com/BadWedding

Bad Engagement
Book Ten
Coming October 12th
www.books2read.com/BadEngagement

ALSO BY ELISE FABER

Billionaire's Club (all stand alone)

Bad Night Stand

Bad Breakup

Bad Husband

Bad Hookup

Bad Divorce

Bad Fiancé

Bad Boyfriend

Bad Blind Date

Bad Wedding (July 19th, 2020)

Bad Engagement (October 12th, 2020)

Chauvinist Stories (all stand alone)

Bitch

Cougar

Whore (May 3rd, 2020)

Love After Midnight (all stand alone)

Rum and Notes

Virgin Daiquiri (June 29th, 2020)

Gold Hockey (all stand alone)

Blocked

Backhand

Boarding

Benched

Breakaway

Breakout

Checked

Coasting (June 15th, 2020)

Life Sucks Series (all stand alone)

Train Wreck

Hot Mess (coming soon)

Roosevelt Ranch Series (all stand alone, series complete)

Disaster at Roosevelt Ranch

Heartbreak at Roosevelt Ranch

Collision at Roosevelt Ranch

Regret at Roosevelt Ranch

Desire at Roosevelt Ranch

Phoenix Series (read in order)

Phoenix Rising

Dark Phoenix

Phoenix Freed

Phoenix: LexTal Chronicles (rereleasing soon, stand alone, Phoenix world)

From Ashes

In Flames

To Smoke

KTS Series

Fire and Ice (Hurt Anthology, stand alone)

Stand Alones

Someday, Maybe (YA)

ABOUT THE AUTHOR

USA Today bestselling author, Elise Faber, loves chocolate, Star Wars, Harry Potter, and hockey (the order depending on the day and how well her team -- the Sharks! -- are playing). She and her husband also play as much hockey as they can squeeze into their schedules, so much so that their typical date night is spent on the ice. Elise changes her hair color more often than some people change their socks, loves sparkly things, and is the mom to two exuberant boys. She lives in Northern California. Connect with her in her Facebook group, the Fabinators or find more information about her books at www.elisefaber.com.

facebook.com/elisefaberauthor

amazon.com/author/elisefaber

bookbub.com/profile/elise-faber

instagram.com/elisefaber

goodreads.com/elisefaber

pinterest.com/elisefaberwrite